Marry for Love

Marry for Love

Christina Courtenay

A Delicious Selection of Bite Size Reads!

Published 2016 by Choc Lit Limited
Penrose House, Crawley Drive, Camberley, Surrey GU15 2AB, UK
www.choc-lit.com

A CIP catalogue record for this book is available
from the British Library

ISBN: 978-1-78189-358-6

Printed and bound by Clays Ltd

Acknowledgements

Huge thanks to my critique partner Gill Stewart who read this at very short notice and whose comments are always spot on!

Many thanks also to the Choc Lit team, my lovely copy editor and most of all the Tasting Panel Members – Hrund, Claire W, Stacey R, Isobel J, Kathleen A, Jo O, Katie P, Gill L, Jenny K, Anja and Prerana – for liking this novella!

Chapter One

Hamish Baillie, fourth earl of Blackwood, stared at the altar and felt the cage closing in on him. It was almost like a physical pain and his sense of being trapped was so acute it made him want to roar with rage and rattle the metaphorical iron bars.

But of course he could do no such thing in this holy place.

'Don't worry, my lord, brides are always a little late. It's their prerogative,' the vicar said, as if he thought the scowl on Hamish's face was because he was being kept waiting. But Hamish wasn't paying much attention to the man. He was too busy inwardly railing at fate.

It was ironic really, he thought, that a man who had managed to avoid the shackles of marriage so successfully for years should have been trapped by a miss barely out of the schoolroom. But her supposed innocence was what had fooled him and lulled him into a false sense of security. He now knew her to be a schemer *extraordinaire* despite her tender years – Wellington himself could have done with some of her stratagems – and he was well and truly caught.

Damnation!

He heard the church door open and glanced down the aisle, bedecked with far more flowers and greenery than one small country church could possibly need. The cloying scent of the roses and lilies alone was enough to make him feel nauseous, it was so overpowering. But then his bride had wanted a society wedding in

St George's Hanover Square, so this was probably her revenge for Hamish's refusal. He noticed that quite a large number of members of the *ton* sat wilting in the pews, even though he'd expressly asked for this to be a small occasion. He would much have preferred not having an audience to witness what some gossips called his 'come-uppance'. Obviously, his wishes didn't enter into the equation here.

His bride entered on her father's arm at last, looking as angelic as the day he'd first set eyes on her. *Angelic, hah!* He doubted she'd ever been sweet in her life. Termagant, more like.

Not wanting to even look at the woman he was about to be tied to for life, he moved his gaze restlessly around the congregation, stopping momentarily when he caught sight of the bride's twin sister. They were uncannily alike and he'd never been able to tell them apart. At the moment, she didn't look much happier than he did, although why that should be so he had no idea. For an instant it made him lower his guard and he allowed the full force of his misery and despair to shine through before shuttering his expression once more. At this sight, the sister looked as though she'd been floored. Her eyes widened and one hand flew up to cover her mouth, but he turned away, no longer wanting to stare at someone so like his future wife.

In fact, he wanted nothing to do with any member of that family, but it would seem he had no choice. He squared his shoulders and tried to resign himself to his fate.

Delilah Risden felt as if someone had punched her right

in the solar plexus. She struggled to breathe, her lungs only slowly drawing in the much needed air, while she blinked at her sister's husband-to-be.

The man had looked positively haunted.

Dear Lord, what was she to do? Lilah couldn't bear to see a human being tortured in this way, forced into doing something that was so wrong. She couldn't allow it to happen, she simply couldn't. She had to stop this marriage, but how?

She racked her brains and bit her lip, staring at the floor while her sister made her way up the aisle as slowly as possible in order to allow everyone to admire her dress. There had been talk of little else for weeks and Lilah was sick of the sight of this garment. And she didn't want to see Deborah's triumphant smile because she knew it was mostly aimed at her, and today it would be worse than ever before.

It had always been the same. Whenever Lilah wanted something, Deborah took it away from her one way or another. Deborah always got her way, by fair means or foul – usually the latter – and Lilah was powerless to stop her. Well, no more. This time her sister had gone too far in trapping an innocent man into marriage just because she had guessed that Lilah was in love with him.

It was all so unnecessary anyway, since Lilah had never had a hope in hell of attracting a man like Lord Blackwood – or Hamish as she secretly called him in her thoughts. Handsome as sin – blond, blue-eyed and with a physique like a Greek god – he could clearly take his pick of the girls on the marriage mart. Lilah hadn't for one instant imagined he'd choose a quiet country girl like herself, despite the fact that she was passably pretty.

Although they had met and spoken a few times, hers had mostly been adoration at a distance and she'd never expected anything to come of it. Deborah, however, was made of sterner stuff and the moment she'd found out about Lilah's *tendre* for the earl, his fate had been sealed.

Ergo, this was all her fault.

It was definitely not right though. Nobody should be made to suffer just because Deborah wanted what Lilah had. Usually the matter remained between the two of them and Lilah put up with that, but involving a third party simply wasn't acceptable. And how was she to survive seeing the couple together at every family occasion for the rest of her life? Watch Deborah lording it over everyone in her role as Countess? Bearing the Earl's children? It would be intolerable. Lilah clenched her jaw and took a deep breath. The time had come for her to act. It was now or never.

Deborah had reached Hamish's side now and Lilah noticed that he couldn't even bring himself to look at his bride. Instead he was studying the fine stained glass windows behind the altar with an intensity that could have burned a hole in them. Deborah's chin shot up a notch and she tossed her head. She obviously thought she would have the last laugh and wasn't bothered about his lack of courtesy.

'I'll soon have the haughty lord tamed and wrapped around my little finger,' Lilah had heard her boasting to her friends. Just the way Deborah had always had her father exactly where she wanted him.

No, I won't allow it, Lilah thought. Enough was enough.

The vicar began the service and after rambling on for a while, he uttered the words Lilah had been waiting for.

'... and if any of you can show just cause why this couple may not lawfully be married, speak now or else forever hold your peace.'

Her body began to shake, but this merely strengthened her resolve. If *she* felt this bad about the marriage, she could only imagine it must be a thousand times worse for Hamish. Although she could never have him herself, she could save him from a fate worse than death, which is what marriage to Deborah would amount to, of that she had no doubt. And she'd save herself from a lifetime of pure misery at the same time.

'I can,' she said in a loud voice and stood up.

A gasp went through the congregation like a gust of wind through a field of ripe corn. She felt, rather than saw, Hamish's gaze come slowly round to settle on her, his blue eyes huge with astonishment, while her mother wheezed in a surprised breath.

'For heaven's sake, child, what are you about? Sit down this instant,' Lady Risden hissed and pulled at Lilah's skirts, but Lilah ignored both her mother's efforts and the fact that her father's countenance had taken on a scowl of monumental proportions.

'I beg your pardon?' The vicar blinked at her, clearly not expecting this.

'There is an impediment to this marriage,' Lilah stated clearly. 'Deborah lied to his lordship to force his hand. In fact, she never spent any time alone with him at all, even though she made him think so. She put laudanum in his tea and when he woke up, she made

5

sure they were found in a compromising position. It was all staged though. I know, because I was there the entire time behind a curtain. So you see, they weren't alone after all.' She ran out of breath and wondered if she'd faint from lack of air.

Exclamations of shock and fierce whispering broke out all around them. This was grist for the gossip mills with a vengeance and Lilah knew there were those among the congregation who would dine out on this tale for weeks to come. She didn't care. Deborah speared her sister with a glance of such venom it ought to have felled her on the spot. Lilah ignored that too and stood her ground.

'She is lying, otherwise why hasn't she said anything before now?' Deborah snarled. 'She's jealous that's all, she always wants what's mine. Besides, it makes no difference either way. Does it?' This last question was fired off at the vicar, who opened and closed his mouth several times, clearly at a loss.

'Well, no, I suppose if ... if you're truly compromised, the fact that there was a witness doesn't ... I mean ...' He faltered.

Hamish had narrowed his eyes at Deborah and crossed his arms over his chest.

'Perhaps we should discuss this?' he suggested, his low voice a menacing rumble.

'There is nothing to discuss. You have asked me to marry you, so let us get on with it,' Deborah said through clenched teeth. 'You cannot go back on your word now. That would be most un-gentlemanly.'

'Wait! There ... there is another impediment.' Lilah could feel little rivulets of perspiration beginning to trickle down her back, but she couldn't back down now. She had to save him before Deborah talked her way out of this. 'He ... that is, his lordship had, er ... c-carnal knowledge of me first.' She felt her face flame, the colour no doubt reaching all the way down her chest and up to her ears, but she carried on in a rush in order to get all the words out before her knees buckled. 'And d-doesn't the Bible say that if a man has lain with one sister, then he cannot marry another? That would be against the laws of consanguinity or something to that effect. Am I right?'

She stared at the vicar, imploring him to help her out and to her relief, his brow furrowed and he nodded. 'Indeed, that is so,' he said. He turned to Hamish. 'Is this true, my lord? You, er ... seduced this young lady's sister first?'

Hamish looked hard at Lilah, his gaze questioning and enigmatic at the same time, and she nodded imperceptibly to show him he should agree. She had already risked so much, one more lie didn't matter.

'Yes,' he said, sounding very convincing and ever so slightly apologetic in a rather haughty and bored way, 'I'm afraid I did.'

Deborah let out a shriek of indignation and slapped him hard across the cheek, but he didn't so much as flinch. Lilah knew it was only a question of time before Deborah's fury would be turned towards her and she therefore hurried to make her way out of the pew and down the aisle as quickly as possible. She held her head high, looking neither right nor left, but she could feel everyone staring as if their eyes pierced her with the needles of their disapprobation. She was officially a

7

fallen woman now, a self-confessed one at that, but she didn't care. After a lifetime of putting up with Deborah's spite and mean tricks, Lilah had finally shown her sister she could only go so far. This marriage was the final straw; Lilah would not allow Deborah to ruin things for her any longer. From now on she would live a life free from her sister and if she had to do it as a servant, so be it. Anything had to be better than this.

And she had saved Hamish – the man she loved – in the process, so perhaps at least one of them could have a happier future.

Hamish gave Deborah a hard stare that dared her to hit him again. Despite being in the throes of a massive temper tantrum, she wisely stuck to screeching. He cut her off in mid-sentence.

'I believe this charade is at an end,' he said and bowed slightly. 'You may keep the vulgar bauble you made me buy you.' He glanced at the huge and tasteless diamond ring on her left hand and knew he'd never want to see it again, much less give it to someone else. 'Good day to you, madam.'

Without another word, he strode out of the church, slamming the doors for good measure, then breathed a sigh of relief so sweet he had never felt its like. He dared not stay where he was, however, in case the hell-cat inside the church managed to think up some other reason why he had to wed her, despite her sister's words. Spying his saviour in the distance, he set out after her at a half-run.

Part-way through a field, he caught up with her.

'Miss Delilah, wait, please.'

She turned and came to a halt, looking up at him with eyes that were uncannily like the silver-coloured pair he'd just left behind in the church, but at the same time vastly different. In their depths he saw no guile, no cunning and no deceit, but that didn't make him trust her. Quite the opposite. He realised now that she was an even better strategist than her sibling and his relief would be of short duration.

'I'm assuming you are now expecting me to marry you instead, so will you do me the honour of becoming my wife?' He said the words in an insolent tone, not bothering to hide his disdain of her tactics. Why should he? She hadn't minced her words in church so she was definitely not missish. 'We'll have to go elsewhere and get a special licence though as I doubt your sister will allow us use of the same church.'

'Thank you, but no. There's no need for that, my lord,' she replied and turned to walk off again. He saw that she was heading for home, albeit via a short-cut across the fields, and soon caught up with her again.

'What do you mean?' he asked, astonished at this turn of events. 'If you're not angling to take your sister's place, why did you tell those lies in church?'

'I simply wanted to free you.'

He raised his eyebrows at her. 'Free me?'

'Yes, from Deborah's clutches. I've suffered her machinations for years, but I saw no reason why you should have to do the same when you'd done nothing to deserve it. She would have made your life a misery. If you'd been a horrid man, I might have stayed silent, but as it was …' She shrugged and carried on walking, but he fell into step beside her.

'So you're saying you ruined your own reputation out of the goodness of your heart in order to save me from your sister? Forgive me if I find that somewhat difficult to believe.'

'Believe what you wish, my lord, it is the truth. And now, if you don't mind, I have things to do.'

They had almost reached the sprawling Tudor manor house that was her home and Hamish looked around him, expecting the wedding party to arrive at any moment and drag him back to his doom. He still couldn't believe that he had escaped. All thanks to the young lady next to him.

'If you don't want to marry me, what *do* you want? Money? Jewels? Marriage to someone else?'

'I want nothing from you and I certainly don't want to marry. My sister would only find some way of enticing any prospective suitor away from me. Please, just leave before it's too late. Trust me, Deborah will think of some way of getting you back if you don't hurry.'

'And what will you do? Surely you cannot stay here now?'

She gave a harsh laugh. 'No, most assuredly not. I shall pack my things and go, as quickly as I can.'

'Go where?'

She threw up her hands. 'I don't know! Somewhere. Anywhere. I'll have to find work of some sort. I don't suppose you know of anyone who needs a companion or governess?' She shook her head. 'No, of course you wouldn't. I doubt you deal with such matters. Never mind.'

He opened his mouth to say no, then remembered something. 'But I do know of someone who needs a housekeeper. Are you any good at domestic matters?'

She laughed again, but it was still not a happy sound. 'Of course. I've been trained to run a household from birth. Where is this position?'

'In Scotland. At my house there, in fact. The old housekeeper died recently and I've yet to replace her. I'll take you on if you wish. I owe you that at least.'

'Your house? But ...'

It was his turn to laugh. 'You don't think it would be seemly for you to work for a single gentleman, is that it? I thought you just told the entire congregation back there that you had shared my bed.'

She blushed bright red and stared at the floor. 'You're right. How silly of me, to be sure.' She looked up again and stared him straight in the eyes. 'Very well, I accept. How do I get there?'

'I'll take you.'

'What? No, that's not necessary. I'm sure I can find my own way if you just tell me how ...'

He took her arm and propelled her towards the front door of the house. 'I'm taking you and that's that. Do you honestly think my other servants would believe you if you arrive to tell them you're the new housekeeper? You look far too young, so it will be up to me to put them right.'

'Oh, I hadn't thought of that.'

'No. It occurs to me you do a lot of acting without thinking things through, although I'm not complaining in this instance, you understand. Let's go and collect your belongings so that we can leave this place. I can't wait to be gone.'

They went into the main hall, startling the butler who was just passing through with a large vase of flowers. He stopped to stare at the pair of them.

'Miss Delilah! But what on earth … Is the service over so soon?'

'No, Jackson, there won't be a wedding today. I'm sorry, I know you've all worked so hard, but there it is. If you'll excuse us?' She turned to Hamish and whispered, 'You can wait in the morning room, I won't be long.'

'The hell I will. I'm coming with you.'

'But you can't—'

'Enter your bedroom?' He raised an eyebrow at her and grinned. 'I thought I already had, although I must have been in my cups since I have no memory of it.'

'Very droll.'

But she didn't protest any further, just led the way to the second floor.

Chapter Two

Lilah's mind was in turmoil, but she knew she couldn't allow herself to think right now, she had to save that for later. At the moment she needed to concentrate on getting out of this place as fast as possible, because there would be hell to pay when her parents returned. Her father would be furious, her mother tearful, and Deborah's methods of revenge were legendary.

'Just take the bare necessities,' Hamish said as soon as the door closed behind him. 'Do you have a horse?' She nodded. 'Then let's ride rather than take a carriage, it will be much faster. If you pack a few essentials into saddle bags, I'll have the rest of your possessions sent for later.'

'Very well.'

Lilah was nothing if not practical and she even had two saddle bags stored in her closet. She pulled them out and started to cram things into them willy-nilly. Yet her brain was strangely clear and she knew that she hadn't forgotten anything vital, despite her haste. In just a few minutes, she had all she needed for a journey.

'Turn around please, I must don my riding outfit.'

'Never mind the prudish act, I'll help you,' he said. 'It's faster that way.'

She had already pulled the garment out of her closet and before she knew it, he was extracting her from her wedding finery. He was so quick with buttons and laces that she had no doubt at all he'd done it before, which only confirmed what she already knew – he was a complete rake. That didn't prevent her from blushing again. She could feel the fiery warmth heating her body as before, but he didn't appear to notice.

He buttoned her into her riding dress and matching jacket at record speed and crammed her small shako onto her head. 'There, you're ready.'

She pushed the saddle bags into his arms and said, 'Not quite. Take those and meet me at the stables. Go down the servants' stairs, first door on your right when you come out of here. Tell Abrams to saddle Nightwish for me as fast as he can – he won't ask any questions. I'll meet you there in a few minutes.'

'But where are you going?'

'To take what's mine.'

Without waiting to see whether he would do as she asked, she left the room and headed for the servants' stairs herself. As yet, she'd heard no sounds of commotion nor any shrieking from the hall, so she knew the rest of the wedding party were not back, but they would be soon. If she hurried, she would have time for what she intended though.

At the back of the hall a door led into her father's study and although he didn't know it, she was well aware of where he kept his strong box and the family's valuables behind a sliding book case. She went there now and didn't hesitate in opening it and reaching for a box with her name on it. It contained all her worldly goods now – the jewels her grandmother had bequeathed to her upon her death – and there was no way she'd leave them behind. She may need to sell them to survive and in any case, Deborah would confiscate them if she could and Lilah refused to let that happen.

She closed the secret hiding place again and left the room. It wasn't a moment too soon, since she heard carriages drawing up on the gravel drive at the front of the house. She sprinted for the green baize door that led to the servants' quarters and after giving a startled Jackson a brief peck on the cheek, she whispered goodbye and headed for the back door.

Hamish was waiting with his own and Delilah's horse just outside the stables. Abrams was with him, making some final adjustments to the saddle, and Hamish saw Delilah go up to him and whisper something in the man's ear. The groom nodded and whispered, 'God go with you, Miss Delilah.' Then he boosted her into the saddle while Hamish mounted his own horse and they were off.

For the first mile they said nothing, merely gave the horses their heads, but when no one appeared to be pursuing them, Hamish slowed down to a canter to give his horse a short break.

'I asked your groom to send a stable boy with a message to my valet at the inn. What did *you* tell him?' he asked as Delilah reined in beside him.

'To say to everyone that you had left the moment you got back from the church, heading for the inn where you were staying, whereas I packed first and then set off in the opposite direction to the one you went.'

'Excellent. Will he do it?'

'Who, Abrams? Of course. He's always been extremely loyal to me. And don't worry, he'll get your message delivered too, discreetly.'

Hamish had gathered as much from the few words

the dour man had let slip. He'd even dared to threaten Hamish on behalf of his mistress. 'If any harm should come to her, there are those here who wouldn't rest until she was avenged,' he'd muttered obliquely. This had amused Hamish at the time since he was sure he could hold his own against a rabble of servants, but he wondered about it now. Had Delilah dallied with the grooms in order to gain her own ends, the way her sister ensnared titled young men? If so, he didn't know which of them was worse.

One thing was certain, however, they seemed cut from the same cloth. If only he knew what Delilah really wanted from him. He was sure that this pretence of only wanting employment wasn't going to last long. Soon, he'd find out her true goal and he had a feeling he wouldn't like it.

'Papa, you must make him come back! Surely there are laws against breaking an engagement? You'll have to threaten to sue him if he refuses to comply.' Deborah stamped her foot on the carpet and let out a theatrical sob. She was still so furious, she didn't have to act much – she really did feel like crying.

'I won't have a leg to stand on if Lilah was telling the truth. The entire congregation will bear witness to her words. Honestly, I cannot believe it of her! How could she do such a thing?' He shook his head and covered his eyes with one hand as if he couldn't bear it. 'The scandal … Does she have no regard for her parents at all? And how could *you* be so stupid as to trick the man? Surely that wasn't necessary? Stealing a *beau* from your sister? You could have had anyone, anyone at all, judging by your success during the season.' Lord Risden paced his study on one side of his desk, while Deborah began to do the same on the other. He had a face like thunder, but that didn't scare her. She knew she could always cajole him into doing what she wanted, but he was being surprisingly obstinate today, just when she needed him most. *Bother!*

'I didn't trick him. Well, not much. It was just a matter of time before he proposed in any case so I just thought I'd hurry matters along a little. Surely that wasn't so wrong?' she wheedled. 'And he wasn't Lilah's *beau*. He never so much as looked at her.'

Her father's scowl didn't let up. 'He's an earl, a peer of the realm. You don't play your silly games with men like that, Deborah. For heaven's sake, what were you thinking?'

She ground her teeth but tried not to scream the way she wanted to. When he called her Deborah rather than 'my sweet', she knew she was in trouble. She had to talk him round in a calm and reasonable manner.

'But Papa, listen I—'

'No, you listen to me for once, my girl. You've made your bed and you must lie in it. There was a long queue of young men falling at your feet, but you had to have the one who wasn't interested. Why? You couldn't bear not to have conquered one of them?'

'No, it wasn't like that, Papa. I fell in love.'

Lord Risden raised his eyebrows in disbelief at this declaration. 'Fustian! You've never been in love in your life. If you had been infatuated with his lordship, you wouldn't have acted the way you did. No, I sense another reason here, but whatever the case, there is nothing we

17

can do about it. We must hope the scandal dies down in a year or so and that some of your faithful admirers will still be willing to propose then. For now, we'll have to stay in the country until the gossip-mongers find something else to tattle about. As for your sister, she is beyond the pale and we will not speak of her. She's no daughter of mine if what she said is true.'

'A year? You mean to keep me here for an entire year? You cannot be serious, Papa. I'll be bored to tears.' Deborah managed to squeeze out a few genuine tears at the thought of being cooped up in Hertfordshire for a whole year, missing the London season and much else besides. But her tears didn't appear to move her father in the slightest, the way they normally would.

'It's no more than you deserve. I've warned you in the past about going too far in the pursuit of your wishes. Now perhaps you'll see the wisdom in my words. Go to your room, Deborah. I wish to be left in peace.' He flapped his hands at her and when she opened her mouth to protest, he said 'Go!' more loudly.

Deborah fled the room, but she wasn't beaten yet. There were other ways of getting what she wanted and if her father wouldn't help her, she'd have to help herself.

'We're sharing a room?'

For the rest of the day they'd ridden as fast as their horses could manage, barely exchanging a word, the urgency of evading any followers spurring them on. Delilah was exhausted from the long ride and the emotions of the morning, but Hamish's casual statement that he'd secured them a room for the night jolted her out of her torpor. The last thing she needed was an argument with him, but she couldn't let this pass.

'Of course we are,' he said with infuriating calm. 'I told the landlord you're my wife.'

'Why? I thought my reputation was already in shreds.' Delilah knew she sounded waspish, but in truth she couldn't help it. The further they had travelled, the more she'd begun to question whether she had taken leave of her senses in risking everything to stand up to her sister and save the man at her side.

He gave her a wry smile now. 'Yours may be, but I'd rather not risk mine too, if you don't mind. I'll have you know I'm a gentleman of honour.'

Lilah sighed. 'Yes, that's what got you into this pickle to begin with.'

Not that his reputation was spotless; far from it if the rumours about him were true. Lilah had been told he was a rake and a gambler, but he'd never compromised any young ladies of virtue, of that she was sure. The matchmaking mothers of the *ton* had been trying to ensnare him for years but he'd steered well clear of any traps. Only Deborah had succeeded, because she was more devious than most people and never played by the rules …

His expression clouded over at her comment and he leaned forward across the table they were sharing in a private parlour. 'Perhaps, but were you telling the truth this morning? Did your sister really give me laudanum?'

'Yes, I'm afraid so.' She looked away, unable to bear the intensity of his gaze. This whole mess was partly her fault after all. If only she'd done something earlier but she had kept quiet as usual thinking there was no point.

A coward, that's what she'd been. Well, no more. Her resolve returned tenfold.

'I suspected foul play of some sort,' Hamish said, 'but I'd had a late night and couldn't be sure it wasn't my own fault I'd fallen asleep in her presence. She must have been very careful as I only nodded off for a few moments. Her maid was there when I drank my tea, but she was gone when I woke up.'

'It was only a drop or two, but it was all she needed. She told the maid to leave as soon as your eyes closed.'

'I did think it strange that her chaperone had disappeared so quickly.'

'Deborah's maid was out of that room in a flash. She'll do anything for money. She's a nasty creature.' Lilah made a face. 'Deborah didn't know that I knew though and I hadn't planned on telling anyone. The scandal ...' She shook her head. Of course she should have told her father right from the start, although he probably wouldn't have believed her. Deborah had him eating out of her hand.

'The scandal is even worse now,' Hamish said, and Lilah knew it was true. But his next words reassured her. 'But I don't give a fig about that, I'm exceedingly grateful to you for rescuing me. Thank you.'

His words sounded as though they were uttered somewhat reluctantly and Lilah saw the mistrust in his eyes. She could understand it. It must seem very strange to him that she should sacrifice her own reputation for his. He'd probably never been in love and nor had he lived for years under the tyranny of someone like Deborah. And now he wouldn't have to.

'You're welcome.' She felt her cheeks heat up,

pleased that at least something good had come of this whole debacle. Then her mind returned to their original debate. 'But really, must we share a room? Can we not have adjoining ones?'

He shook his head. 'I'm sorry, the inn is full. Besides, I'd like you nearby in case of trouble.'

She blinked. 'T-trouble? You mean, you still think they'll find us and drag me back?'

'I doubt it, but just in case, I've bribed one of the landlord's sons to warn us if anyone comes asking questions. That will give us time to escape. And he's to keep the horses in the paddock behind the stables so that no one sees them if they arrive unexpectedly.'

'Oh, well, good.'

He'd thought of everything and it seemed churlish to argue about where they were to sleep.

'How much do I owe you for the meal?' Lilah picked up her reticule from the table and opened it to dig around for her small purse. She had been saving her pin money for quite some time as she wasn't as fond of fripperies as her sister, so she was sure she would have enough to reimburse Hamish for what she had eaten.

He stared at her as if she'd suddenly sprouted wings. 'Owe me?'

'Yes, for the food. And you must let me pay for my share of the room cost.' She waved her purse at him. 'I'm not entirely without means yet.'

Hamish blinked and shook his head. 'There's no need. You're my employee now. I'll take care of it.'

'But I haven't started work yet and I don't wish to be beholden …'

He held up his hand to stop her. 'Keep your coins. You may need them in the future.' When she opened her mouth to argue further, he added sternly, 'I mean it. Now let's go to bed.'

Lilah felt her eyelids drooping. She was too tired to protest further and if he wanted to waste his money on her, then why not let him? 'Very well. Thank you.'

'Come, you're almost asleep on your feet.' Hamish stood up and held out a hand to help her out of her chair. She put hers into his larger one and he tucked it into the crook of his arm, leading her to the door. The sensation of his muscular arm beneath her fingers, even through the layers of clothing, was most unsettling. She had to suppress a shiver when he bent to whisper, 'You have nothing to fear from me tonight, you have my word. I'm as tired as you are. Now pretend you're my wife, we don't want to rouse anyone's suspicions.'

Lilah glanced up at him and saw that he appeared sincere. His words disturbed her nonetheless. He'd only said 'tonight', which implied she may not be safe thereafter, but for now, she had to make do with this.

'I'll wait in the corridor while you prepare yourself for bed.'

Hamish left her kneeling next to one of her saddle bags and went to stand outside the door. It was silly really, since he'd already helped her change her clothes that morning, but he could see that she was very tired now and thought it best not to rile her. He hoped she wouldn't take forever though and that she was able to cope without the help of a maid. He'd had to lie to the landlady when she offered the use of a serving wench and say that as they were newlyweds he preferred to help his wife himself.

Better not to let anyone see how light Delilah was travelling. He'd have to buy her some more clothes along the way.

'Delilah,' he murmured. Since when had he started to think of her by her first name? It should be 'Miss Delilah' at the very least, since her sister as the eldest would be Miss Risden. But he was so sick of the sound of that particular surname, he much preferred Delilah. And surely they'd gone beyond mere politeness?

He couldn't make her out. All day he'd waited to hear some ultimatum or other from her, but she'd not said a word. Valiantly, she had kept up with him, even when he could see she was flagging, and she never uttered so much as the smallest complaint. And what of her offer to pay for her food and lodging? He'd been so surprised he was lost for words momentarily. He'd expected her to try to milk him of every penny she could and yet she'd pulled out her meagre purse with what looked like steely determination.

She was definitely the complete opposite to her sister. *Or an even better actress?*

At the thought of the girl he'd escaped marrying that morning, a shudder passed through him. It would have been a most uncomfortable union, of that he was certain. Deborah Risden was not someone you could trust and Hamish knew he would have spent the rest of his life living on tenterhooks. Not to mention keeping an eye on his fortune, which Deborah would definitely have tried to spend at every turn. He'd already had a taste of her extravagant ways when she'd demanded that huge diamond ring and a number of other gifts in the run-up to the wedding.

He thought back to that fatal afternoon, when he'd fallen asleep in the back parlour of the Risden town house, a small cosy room normally used by the ladies of the house when they were on their own, to judge by the sewing paraphernalia and ladies' magazines strewn about the room.

'I do apologise for receiving you in here, Lord Blackwood,' Deborah had said, 'but the best parlour is being redecorated at the moment.'

Hamish hadn't seen any evidence of that, but then all the other doors leading to the hall had been closed and he hadn't been invited up to the first floor of the house so he'd swallowed her lie. He should have been on his guard after that, but the hangover from the night before had made it hard to think, never mind react.

He had tried half-heartedly to leave. 'I just came to pay a morning call. Perhaps another time?' he'd said.

He had been to the house a couple of times before. Even though he wasn't really interested in her as a prospective wife there was no harm in letting other men see that he could attract someone if he wanted to. The place was usually crawling with love-sick young men and it had amused him to be singled out by Miss Risden during such visits. On this occasion he was the only one there and alarm bells should have rung loud and clear at that point. What a fool he'd been.

He could only blame that infernal headache. Why else would he have accepted the offer of a dish of tea? He should have left the moment he saw that no one else was there …

Thank the Lord he had been spared from marrying Miss Risden after all. But what awaited him instead?

The door behind him opened a fraction now, revealing the person who might hold his future in her hands. 'I'm ready. Give me a moment and I'll jump under the covers,' Delilah whispered.

Hamish took a deep breath, waited a little longer, then entered the bed chamber, locking the door behind him. There was only one candle lit and the fire in the hearth had died down to smouldering embers. This made it seem very cosy and intimate, which wasn't what he'd expected. It set his nerves on edge.

He sat down on his side of the bed and began to pull off his Hessian boots, wishing he hadn't had to leave his valet behind. But at least he always had a couple of spare shirts and neck cloths in his own saddle bags, an old habit he had cause to be grateful for now.

'Are you comfortable?' he asked, just for something to say. He needed to make small talk in order to break the tension he could feel reverberating around the room. What was he doing, putting himself in this situation? Sharing a bed with Delilah for a whole night, however innocently, was tantamount to giving her permission to force him into wedlock. Exactly the way her sister had done. Out of the frying pan and into the fire?

'Perfectly, thank you.' Her muffled reply made him realise she had burrowed as far under the bedclothes as she possibly could, but he still heard a slight quiver in her voice.

'Are you afraid of me?' he asked, astonished. She'd been so courageous the rest of the day, it seemed strange to think she was scared of sleeping in here with him.

'No, certainly not.'

Hamish smiled to himself, recognising bravado when he heard it. 'I told you, there's no need. We'll put a bolster between us and I give you my oath as a gentleman I won't cross that dividing line.' A little devil made him add, 'Unless you want me to?'

He heard a small gasp. 'No! I mean, you said …'

He chuckled and put out a hand to pat the covers next to him. 'I know. I'm roasting you. Sorry, that was not well done but I couldn't resist.' He blew out the candle and stretched out next to her, fully clothed, pulling a spare blanket over himself.

'Oh.'

Was that disappointment? Had she expected him to make love to her so that she'd definitely be compromised, even though she was clearly afraid? He couldn't be sure. He'd never spent the night with a virgin so had no idea how one would react. Either way, he'd meant what he said, he wouldn't be touching her tonight. 'Goodnight, Delilah,' he murmured.

'Goodnight, er, Hamish.'

For some reason, hearing her say his name in the dark made him feel all warm inside, but he quashed this and closed his eyes.

Chapter Three

'Where has she gone, the worthless, conniving little baggage? And don't waste my time by saying you don't know, Abrams, because I know you'd be lying.'

Deborah felt red-hot fury still coursing through her veins as she faced the head groom. It hadn't abated one iota since the previous morning when her sister had ruined what was supposed to have been the greatest triumph of Deborah's life so far. The moment when she became the Countess of Blackwood.

Instead, here she was, a laughing stock and still without a title and rich husband. All because of Lilah, the treacherous bitch.

Deborah had never imagined her sister would have it in her to do something like this, otherwise she would have taken measures to prevent her from attending the wedding. She had, foolishly as it turned out, thought to show Lilah how worthless she was by allowing her to watch. Seeing her timid twin's expression as Deborah married the man she loved would have been the icing on the cake. But somehow, the mouse had turned into a lion.

Deborah had obviously underestimated Lilah's love for the Earl and her determination. She wouldn't make that mistake again.

'Abrams!' she screeched, slapping the man's impassive face and stamping her foot. 'Tell me or so help me, I'll make life very difficult for you.'

'I'm sorry, Miss Risden, but she didn't inform me.

Just said to saddle her horse in a great hurry and took off.'

'Twaddle!'

'It's the truth, Miss. There wasn't time for any chatting. Miss Delilah seemed … desperate, like.'

That rang true and made Deborah hold back from slapping the annoying man again. Lilah must have known she'd ruined herself, as well as the whole family, by causing such a scandal. She would have been running from their father's wrath, not just Deborah's. But still …

She narrowed her eyes at the groom.

'At least tell me in which direction she went. I'm sure you saw that much.'

'Miss Delilah went south-east, Miss Risden. If I may hazard a guess, she was heading for London.'

As the Risden estate was situated in Hertfordshire, Deborah agreed with the groom's assessment. Besides, it would make sense for Lilah to go to the capital. She'd need to find employment of some sort and that was where all the agencies for such things were to be found. Unless there was some relative or friend she could take refuge with? But Deborah couldn't think of anyone who'd take Lilah in under the circumstances.

It gave her some satisfaction to think of her sister having to work for a living – it was no more than she deserved – but at the same time she wanted to be the one meting out a suitable punishment. She couldn't let her twin get away so easily. Another thought occurred to her.

'And Lord Blackwood, which way did he go?'

'Back to the inn, Miss. To collect his things, most like. Took off like he had the devil on his tail.'

'Very well. You may go for now, but if I find that you've been lying to me ...' She left the sentence hanging, hoping to intimidate the man, but to her annoyance he remained stony-faced. He'd ever been a thorn in her side but since he was such a good groom she hadn't been able to persuade her father to part with the man. She'd have to find a way.

For now, she had other more important things to do. 'Saddle my horse,' she commanded.

She'd go to the inn just to make sure his lordship hadn't gone anywhere with her sister.

Lilah woke early but feeling more rested than she had in a long while. Her worries about the wedding had given her sleepless nights and she realised this was the first time in ages she'd slept like a log. It was strange, but she'd felt safe next to Hamish, trusting him. And he'd been true to his word, staying on his side of the bed outside the blankets.

Good.

She ignored the treacherous little voice inside her head which was wishing he'd at least tried to persuade her into sharing the bed properly. Although she was officially a fallen woman, there was no need for her to act like one, tempting though that may be. Lilah gave herself a stern reprimand.

You are the Earl's employee now – or soon will be – and have no business thinking of him in any other terms. He will never see you as anything other than a servant at best and a nuisance at worst.

She must put all thoughts of love from her mind.

To her relief, Hamish wasn't in the room and she

hurried into her clothes, grateful for the privacy. When she came downstairs, he was waiting in the private parlour and Delilah ate quickly, sensing his impatience to be off.

They headed north-east for a while, in order to confuse anyone who might be following, then north-west.

'Where is your estate exactly?' Lilah asked.

'It's on the west side of Scotland, just above Loch Lomond. We are heading for Carlisle first, then we'll continue north from there.'

This explanation didn't mean much to her, as she'd never been to Scotland, but she supposed she'd just have to wait and see. In any case, she gathered it would take them quite some time to reach their destination.

When Hamish deemed it safe, they stopped at a large town and had luncheon in one of the smaller inns.

'No point going into the coaching inn at the centre of town,' he explained. 'That'll be the first place they'll look for someone like me.'

'Yes, that makes sense.' Lilah nodded. 'I dare say you're used to the best wherever you go.'

He shot her a look which she couldn't quite read, but said only, 'Just so.'

After a light meal, Hamish suggested they leave their horses and walk for a bit. 'I need to buy a few supplies,' he said, 'as I didn't get a chance to pack.'

He purchased several shirts, cravats and various other necessary items, before continuing. In one of the streets off the main square, he spotted a small dressmaker's shop which he pointed out to Lilah. 'Let us go and see whether they have any gowns suitable for a housekeeper. I doubt you own anything dour enough.'

'But ...' Lilah swallowed her protest. He was right after all. The clothes she had packed were not suitable for a servant, however high-ranking. They'd been made for her London season. 'Very well, but I doubt they'll have anything ready-made.'

In this she was proved wrong. When asked whether she happened to have any finished gowns, preferably in black or dark colours, the proprietor said, 'Yes, I have two dresses that were made recently for a widow, but she succumbed to a fever herself before she was able to collect them. Let me show you.'

She fetched one dress of shining blue-black silk, which rustled whenever it was handled, and one of good quality black wool. 'Will these do? Of course, they'll probably have to be altered, as you are much smaller, my lady. We can help with that unless your servants can see to it?'

It took Lilah a moment to realise the woman meant her when she said 'my lady'. Hamish had told the dressmaker they were on their way to someone's deathbed, in a hurry, and needed something suitable for after their relative's demise.

'I'm sure my servants can see to it, thank you,' Delilah said with as much composure as she could muster. 'Will these do, er, husband dear?' she asked Hamish.

She saw his eyes glint with humour for a moment, but he nodded solemnly. 'They'll have to as we can't afford to waste any more time.' He turned to the dressmaker. 'If you'd be so kind as to wrap these up quickly, we'd be much obliged. And perhaps you could add some needle and thread, please, just in case the servants forgot to bring some?'

They were soon on their way again, having retrieved their horses and tied the parcel of dresses to Lilah's saddle.

'Will you be able to alter these yourself, do you think?' Hamish asked. 'I'd rather you wore one of them when we arrive so as to make the right impression from the start. I can order you better ones when you're settled, but until then these will have to do.'

'Thank you, yes, I'll work on them in the evenings. It shouldn't be a problem. And thank you again for paying. You must take it out of my wages eventually.'

'Nonsense. I'm sure most employers provide clothing for their servants, I certainly do. I'll hear no more about that.'

In truth, Hamish was even more perplexed than before. He'd been sure that once he took her to a dressmaker's, Delilah would somehow cajole him into buying her all manner of things. Ladies always seemed to need just one more cloak, Spencer, shift or a pair of silk stockings, and he was expected to pay. To his astonishment, Delilah hadn't asked for a thing. He'd had to almost force her to add extra undergarments – as Scotland was cold for most of the year – stockings and a shawl. And now she wanted to pay for it herself?

Unheard of.

Either she really was playing a very deep game, or she was genuinely different to her sister. He found that he was hoping it was the latter, since he was beginning to enjoy spending time with her. She was quick-witted and had a sense of humour which shone through every now and then when she allowed herself to relax a little in his company. He began to look forward to those moments.

'Tell me about your London season,' he said, in order to encourage her to talk a bit more about herself. He found to his surprise that he wanted to get to know her. *Well, better the devil you know and all that.* But he had to acknowledge to himself that he was having more and more trouble seeing her as evil. She seemed so very different to her sister.

She made a face. 'You mean Deborah's season, don't you?'

'No, I want to know about yours. You came out at the same time, obviously – or didn't you?'

'Yes, but I may as well not have.' With a deprecating smile and a shrug she explained further. 'Deborah always saw to it that she was the centre of attention. I was allowed to dance with anyone she didn't have time for at that precise moment, but she'd charm them again if they showed even the slightest interest in pursuing me instead.' Delilah sighed. 'That's just the way she is.'

Hamish frowned. 'But that's dreadful! Surely your parents don't stand for that sort of behaviour?' He wasn't sure he believed it. He knew Deborah was capable of acting thus, but from what he'd seen of Delilah, she could more than hold her own.

'I don't think they really noticed. Mama was so pleased at what she called our success, she didn't pay attention. And there has never been any point in my complaining about Deborah. She manages to weasel her way out of any accusation and turn it around so that I'm the one to blame. It's a particular skill of hers.

If all else fails, she pretends to *be* me and most people fall for that as we're so alike.'

'Even your mother and father? I thought parents of twins could always tell them apart.'

'They can if we're standing next to each other, but not when Deborah deliberately imitates me. I do have a small scar here, just under my jaw line.' Delilah rode closer and lifted up her chin to show a very faint white hairline scar. Hamish could just about make it out at that distance. 'But they seldom think to look for that and with Deborah playing the role of me so well, why would they?'

'Sounds outrageous to me,' Hamish muttered.

'Well, you should know what she's like. You fell foul of it too,' Delilah pointed out.

'True. And I thought I knew every trick in the book. I'd just never realised someone so young and innocent-looking could be such a schemer. It was the slightly more mature girls I was wary of. They had a certain look in their eyes which I came to recognise.'

'Yes, well, now you know you can be on your guard in future.'

'You may be sure I shall. And I won't mistake you for your sister in future.'

Lilah couldn't help but smile at his certainty and tease him a little. 'Like you did before, you mean?'

'I beg your pardon?'

'You danced with me in London, thinking I was Deborah. I thought you'd realise you had the wrong sister when you commented on how quiet I was that evening, but you never did.'

To Lilah that night was etched in her memory as one of the best in her life. Hamish had danced with her twice – a heavenly sensation since one of the dances was a waltz – then taken her in to supper. They'd joined a crowd of his friends who laughed and joked with each other. Lilah had felt included and although not as vociferous as the others, she'd done her best to join in, fantasising about what it would be like to be Hamish's partner at every ball.

But just like Cinderella's, her evening had ended abruptly when Deborah claimed a headache and her Mama had come to retrieve her.

'When was this? Oh, wait, I remember – the Sutton's ball, wasn't it? That was you?' Hamish frowned. 'But you never said ...'

'That I wasn't Deborah? No, she'd have made me pay for it, I knew that.' Lilah shrugged. In truth, she had toyed with the idea of telling him, but she'd been aware he was only flirting with her out of habit. 'Besides, would it have made a difference? You weren't hanging out for a wife, I could tell.'

'No, you're right. I ... hadn't considered matrimony urgent as yet. I'm not exactly in my dotage.' He gave her a lop-sided smile.

He was twenty-seven. Lilah knew because she'd made it her business to find out. Plenty of time for him to marry and sire an heir, after enjoying life first. She'd been prepared to wait until he *was* in the market for a wife, then she could have tried her best to capture him. She probably wouldn't have had any chance of success, but either way Deborah had found out about her infatuation and taken matters into her own hands ...

'How come your sister allowed you to dance with me that time?' Hamish asked.

'Deborah was busy flirting with the Duke of Alderney. Becoming a duchess would obviously have been even more of a feather in her cap.' Lilah sent Hamish an apologetic glance, but he was a man of the world and he'd know there were women who married only for the highest title. It wasn't uncommon.

'I take it she caught cold at that,' he commented wryly.

Lilah nodded. 'Yes, it only took her half an evening before she realised that particular duke was never going to fall for her wiles.'

'Er, quite so.' Hamish coughed.

Lilah could feel a blush creep up her neck. It had taken her a bit longer to hear the rumours of Alderney's preference for young boys. 'It was very early in the season and we hadn't been in town for very long at that point.' Which explained Deborah's mistake. Lilah was grateful for it though as it had given her the opportunity to spend time with Hamish. Thank goodness the duke had been amused enough at Deborah's attempt to keep stringing her along for at least a while.

'Were there any other times?'

'I'm sorry, what?' Lilah shook herself inwardly and tried to stop day-dreaming. She had to forget those memories. It would only hurt more if she allowed herself to think of such wonderful moments.

'Did I ever mistake you for your sister again after that?'

'Oh, uhm ...' Another fiery blush heated Lilah's cheeks and she looked away. 'On a couple of occasions, yes.'

'When?'

She could feel his gaze boring into the back of her head, but she couldn't face him. Or tell him the truth.

'Just a few times when my sister was busy. You came for tea once, after the engagement had been announced, and she had a dress fitting which she couldn't postpone ...'

And then there was that other time, when Lilah had bumped into him in Lady Garside's conservatory. He'd been half-cut and flirtatious, stealing a brief kiss behind a plant, his lips soft and tasting of brandy ... But there was no way she would mention that.

When she was sure her cheeks had cooled a bit, she turned to face him again and saw him watching her with narrowed eyes, but he didn't press her for more information.

Perhaps he didn't want to remember.

'His lordship didn't come back here at all? You are sure?'

Deborah smelled a rat and she wanted answers. The surly landlord of the Stag Inn hadn't wanted to speak to her at all, but a golden guinea soon loosened his tongue although Deborah was annoyed at having to part with so much of her pin money. She'd already had to bribe Dawson, her maid, to accompany her without telling anyone where they were going.

'I swear it. I'd have seen him, wouldn't I? It's not as if 'e's hard to miss, that one.'

That was true. Tall and formidable, with golden hair and deep blue eyes, Lord Blackwood was certainly memorable. Seeing as there was a lack of marriageable dukes at the moment, Deborah would probably have picked him as her future husband even if Lilah hadn't already fallen for the man. That simply made ensnaring him that much more fun. But had her twin had the last laugh? She couldn't bear that thought.

'Did my sister pass this way? I believe she's on her way to London so should have ridden past.'

The landlord shook his head. 'Didn't see hide nor hair of 'er, Miss. All I know is a note was d'livered for 'is lordship's valet, who packed up and left in a great hurry. Paid 'andsomely and all, didn't even argue 'bout the amount. You'd have thought the devil hisself was after 'im.'

'And where was he going? To Lord Blackwood's Wiltshire estate?'

'Don't think so. Lunnon way, I reckon. He headed south-east.'

Deborah scowled. So if his lordship was heading for London as well, he could be escorting Lilah, who may have taken a different route so no one would see them together. That wasn't something she could allow. Lilah wasn't scintillating company like herself, but Deborah knew there were men who preferred that type of meek, biddable creature and Lilah was a past master at acting that part. Lord Blackwood could fall for the "sweet little innocent" posturing along the way.

There was nothing for it – Deborah had to go after them and at least retrieve her sister, if not her former husband-to-be.

It was a dashed nuisance, but what choice did she have?

Chapter Four

'Hamish, are you there?'

The soft knock on his door and hissed whisper startled Hamish as he'd been standing by the window thinking of Delilah. It was as if his thoughts had conjured her up.

He opened his door a fraction and peered out, noting that there was no one else about. 'Yes? Is something amiss?'

'Er, no, not exactly, but I … I'm afraid I need your help. Could you possibly come into my room for a moment? Without anyone seeing you of course.'

Hamish wanted to say no as he definitely didn't want to go anywhere near her bed chamber, but if she genuinely needed help, how could he refuse?

'Give me a minute and I'll be there,' he replied gruffly and shut the door on her while he went to pull on his boots.

Damnation, what was she up to now? Had she decided to entice him into sharing a room with her after all? Well, she'd catch cold at that as he would remain firm, especially as this time he'd managed to find an inn with two available rooms.

Her door was slightly ajar so he entered quickly and shut it before anyone else appeared on the landing. He turned around and was astonished to find Delilah standing on a chair. 'What the devil …? I mean, beg your pardon, but what on earth are you doing?'

Delilah giggled, a delightful sound that almost had

him reaching up to put his hands round her tiny waist and lifting her down into his arms.

'I'm sorry, it must look a bit odd,' she said. 'But it's necessary. I need your help to pin up my hem. Would you mind? I simply can't manage it on my own, at least not if it's to be straight.'

'Oh, I see. Well, I can't say I've ever done it before so it may not be any straighter, but I'll give it a try.'

'Thank you. Here, take these.' She bent down to hand him a paper full of pins which the dressmaker must have included when they bought the dress.

Hamish saw now that she was wearing the black silk and it seemed to fit her perfectly everywhere else, hugging her delightful curves. He looked away from those, tempting as they were. Her stunning figure was one of the reasons he'd spent any time at all in Deborah's company – and Delilah's apparently – during the season, even though he normally stayed away from the debutantes. And look where that had led him …

'So you've managed to alter it?' he asked, kneeling on the floor beside her and grabbing a handful of material.

'Yes, I had no trouble with that. It's just the hem which I can't reach myself. No, wait, not like that. Like this, if you please.' She showed him how to fold the material up twice and make it even, or as even as he could possibly manage, which probably wasn't perfect.

Hamish worked his way round the bottom of her gown, getting more than one glimpse of her slim ankles and dainty feet. She was only wearing stockings, no shoes, and seeing her like that felt incredibly intimate, even though she was fully dressed and no skin was on display. He shook his head at himself. He must be going soft in the head if he was admiring her feet now. *Struth!*

'There, all done,' he declared and stood up. Without thinking, he reached up his hands and lifted her off the chair, setting her down right in front of him. Her chest brushed against his, sending a frisson of desire shooting through him. They were standing so close he could see every tiny freckle on her nose and he had a sudden urge to kiss every one of them. He took a step back in order to put some distance between them. This wouldn't do.

'Thank you, but would you mind doing the other one as well, please?'

'What?'

Hamish had still been trying to conquer his desire to kiss her and at first her question didn't penetrate.

'The other gown, the woollen one – it needs to be hemmed up too. Will you help me?'

Lilah was looking up at him with those extraordinary eyes, like silvery diamonds, and although he knew it would be better if he left right now, he found it hard to refuse. 'Very well,' he said.

'Then close your eyes for a moment, please.'

He did as she asked, but as he listened to the shushing noise of the silk material when she discarded the first gown, he had to clench his fists to stop himself from peeking. He'd seen her in her shift once before and had no trouble recalling what she looked like, but he'd dearly like to see her that way again.

He shouldn't. He mustn't. *I must stay strong.*

So far she'd stuck to her word and made no demands upon him, other than wanting to be employed as his housekeeper. If there was any chance that she was genuinely only asking for that much, he couldn't afford to compromise her any further than was necessary.

But, dear Lord, he so wanted to kiss her.

Lilah leaned against the door after she'd bolted it shut behind Hamish's retreating back. She found that she was shaking, just from having been in the same room as him. And that moment when they'd been standing so close, she'd thought he was going to kiss her and … Lord help her, but she'd wanted him to. Properly this time, not like that quick chaste kiss in Lady Garside's conservatory.

She was in a bad way.

But if nothing else, this proved that she really did love the man and in setting him free from her sister, she'd done the right thing. At least now he could make his own choice of wife, without being forced in any way. Hopefully he'd find a woman who would make him happy. Someone worthy of being his countess.

She put her forehead against the cool wood of the door frame. He'd asked *her* to marry him, there in the field when he'd come running after her out of the church. If only she could have said yes. Her whole being had cried out for her to do so, but her pride forbade it. She wouldn't have been any better than her sister if she'd accepted. And he would have resented her, perhaps even hated her, for the rest of his life.

No, if she was ever to marry – and that seemed unlikely now – it would be to someone who truly wanted her.

Sadly, that would never be Hamish.

* * *

They continued northwards, with a few small detours to the east and west from time to time. Hamish didn't think anyone was actually following them, apart from hopefully his valet who, with a bit of luck, would reach Scotland before them if he travelled in a straight line. Still, it was best to be vigilant. Delilah seemed afraid her father would pursue them in order to punish her, and Hamish himself would rather not see Lord Risden again for the foreseeable future.

He'd decided they should travel under a false name – Mr and Mrs Robarts – never stopping at inns where he'd been before. 'Our fake identities might not fool anyone for long, but it could help confuse any pursuers for a while at least,' he told Delilah.

'I suppose you are right.' She seemed relieved not to have to share a bed chamber with him, while he found it more and more difficult to sleep, knowing she was so near. He had to admit now that he was extremely attracted to her, but since he still wasn't convinced she could be trusted, there was no way he would let her know that.

Delilah was a very beautiful young lady, there was no doubt about it. That was, after all, why he'd been taken in by her sister in the first place to the extent that she managed to dupe him. Thick, brown hair, as lustrous as polished oak with a hint of chestnut, and sparkling quicksilver eyes framed with long, dark lashes made for an enchanting first impression. Just like Deborah, he'd discovered Delilah had dimples on either side of the full mouth and that tiny sprinkling of freckles across the small straight nose. When quizzed about these, Delilah admitted that ordinarily she and her sister would hide them with rice powder.

'For you know, freckles are not at all the thing,' she said with a smile that showed she was repeating something she'd been told but thought ludicrous. 'Although when riding like this, I don't suppose they matter much. And in any case, no one will care whether a housekeeper has them or not, will they?'

Hamish could have told her they mattered a lot, since the sight of them made her look more vulnerable and entirely too enticing for her own good. He doubted anyone in the entire country had a housekeeper as young and pretty as her. How in the world was he going to convince the rest of his staff that's what she was? They'd think she was his mistress for sure.

And hell, she was only nineteen.

He groaned inwardly.

As they entered the tap room of a small inn somewhere near the Lake District – or so Hamish had said – Lilah became aware that a silence descended on the room almost immediately. It was dark in there, with only the light from a fire and a few smoking candles shining through the gloom, but she sensed eyes watching her even though she couldn't see them.

'What can I do for ye?' The landlord came forward, dragging his feet as if he was reluctant to serve them. He didn't bow the way most innkeepers would either. Lilah's stomach gave a nervous flutter.

She noticed him throwing an anxious glance towards one corner of the room where suppressed guffaws of laughter emanated from a trio of unkempt men. One in particular seemed to be throwing them malevolent glances and she suppressed a shudder.

Hamish appeared unaffected. 'I'd like two of your best chambers, please, my good man, and some supper for my wife and myself,' he said in a commanding, but pleasant, voice.

'Very well, the missus'll see to it.' The landlord beckoned to a small, thin woman who was cowering behind the counter. 'Mary, you heard the man. Stir yerself.'

The woman scurried away and Hamish guided Lilah towards a seat near the fireplace. This happened to be next to where the group of men were sitting and as Lilah came closer, the malevolent one stood up and sneered, looking her up and down before addressing Hamish.

'We don't want the likes of you round 'ere. Why don't you go off to the White Hart, same as all the other fancy gents?'

Hamish's hand slipped round Delilah's shoulder in a protective grasp. 'Perhaps we prefer the comforts of this inn. What's it to you?'

'Braithwaite, no trouble now, please,' the innkeeper called out, but the man ignored him and took another step closer, his gaze menacing.

'I said, this 'ere's our inn and we don't want it polluted by the high-falutin' likes of you.'

Delilah felt Hamish stiffening at her side and he slowly manoeuvred her so that she was behind him. 'The way I see it, it's a free country, and if I wish to stay here that's my prerogative. Now why don't you get back to your ale and leave me and my wife in peace, hmm?'

'"Perogative",' Braithwaite tried to imitate Hamish's accent, then laughed. 'Hark at him! Ain't no such thing. We were 'ere first. Now go!'

'Are you going to make me?' Hamish's voice was silken but with an underlying menace that matched Braithwaite's.

'Now Braithwaite, I've told ye before …' The landlord tried to defuse the situation, but didn't show any signs of coming forward to actually help.

Lilah could see why. Braithwaite was a big man with a half-bald head and well-muscled arms. She sidled away from him, towards the fireplace, but didn't want to leave Hamish completely.

'Yes, I'll make ye,' Braithwaite said, a cock-sure glint in his eyes. He was obviously spoiling for a fight.

'Then try.' Hamish sounded so unafraid Delilah couldn't believe it. How could he be so calm? There were three thugs, one of them the huge Braithwaite, and only one of him. Was he mad?

As Braithwaite lunged at Hamish, Lilah looked around for some kind of weapon or another way of helping him. The landlord was obviously not going to be of any use as he was just wringing his hands, while the other occupants of the room either cowered in their own corners or looked on with smiling faces, enjoying the fight. It was up to Lilah to find a solution.

Hamish seemed to be holding his own, at first against just Braithwaite, then when they noticed their leader didn't immediately triumph, the other two who joined in. Although he was obviously good with his fists, Lilah didn't think Hamish could possibly beat all three at once so she rushed over to the fireplace and grabbed the first thing she could find – a thick iron poker.

Braithwaite was just about to hit Hamish when Lilah crept up behind him and whacked him across the back of the skull with the poker as hard as she could. She saw his eyes turn up until only the whites were showing, then he crashed to the floor. His companions stopped to stare at him in stunned silence, giving Hamish the opportunity to smash his fist into first one, then the other's jaw. It was only a matter of moments before all three were lying senseless on the floor.

Barely panting from the effort, Hamish turned to Delilah. 'Thank you for your assistance. I believe I had the situation under control, but you certainly speeded things up.' He smiled. 'I shall make sure never to get in the way whenever you wield a poker in future.'

'I ... you're welcome.' She found that she was shaking and sank onto the nearest bench. 'I believe I could do with a brandy now. If you please?'

Hamish burst out laughing. 'Landlord, you heard my wife – a glass of your finest brandy, please!'

He hunkered down in front of Lilah and whispered. 'And then we'll leave. I apologise for exposing you to such a dangerous situation, my mistake. I'll choose inns more wisely in future, I promise.'

Hamish was cross with himself. He hadn't been worried about the fight as such, since the three men were all clearly half-drunk and therefore slow in their reflexes. He would have beaten them fairly easily, he was sure. But he should have chosen an inn with more care so that Delilah wouldn't have had to witness such a thing, let alone feel obliged to take part. They'd had a particularly long day in the saddle and he'd known Lilah was exhausted, which was why he hadn't bothered to search for a better inn. He should have done. He'd had a bad feeling the minute they walked into that tap room, but by then it had been too late.

He'd put her in danger. That thought made him go cold.

However, he'd never backed down from an encounter in his life and there was no way he'd allow a bully like Braithwaite to intimidate him. He'd rather have been beaten senseless, but for the first time in his life he'd had someone else depending on him too. The rush of protectiveness he'd felt for Delilah as the man threatened them was overwhelming and not a little frightening.

She'd been terrified, he'd seen it in her eyes and felt her quivering slightly, but she'd neither run away, screamed nor had a fit of the vapours. Instead she'd taken matters into her own hands.

Hamish couldn't help but admire her courage and he realised it wasn't something she could have faked. It was real. She'd joined in the fight to help him, without expecting him to either bribe their way out of the situation or protect her. He was totally sure her sister would never have acted thus.

How could he continue to mistrust Delilah's motives when she showed such bravery? Had he misjudged her?

He didn't know what to think, but right now, he wanted her safe.

Lilah opened her eyes the next morning and found herself face to face with Hamish, whose blue eyes, only inches away, blinked as if he too had just awoken. They'd found another inn, but there had only been one room available, forcing them to share yet again.

'Good morning.'

His slow smile at such close quarters would have floored her if she hadn't already been lying down. He was devastatingly handsome, even with his blond hair tousled and stubble on his chin, and she was suddenly extremely conscious of his long limbs lying so close to her own. The bedclothes still separated them in theory, just like on that first night, but they might as well not have been there for all she noticed them. She'd never been so aware of another human being in her life.

Lilah was just about to reply but didn't get the chance as he leaned forward and kissed her. It was deliberate – his soft mouth had been aiming for hers, no doubt about it. Lilah froze, unable to move so much as a muscle while his lips caressed hers. It felt wonderful, this small touch sending waves of awareness right down to her toes, but she didn't reciprocate. She couldn't; didn't know how even if she'd wanted to. Which she most certainly didn't, right?

But she did.

Dear Lord, she was allowing him to kiss her, which was tantamount to an invitation to … she drew in a sharp breath and sat up. 'Hamish! I mean … my lord, you said you wouldn't …'

He sat up too, throwing off the blanket, and held up his hands in a gesture of peace. 'I'm sorry. I know, I shouldn't have done that, but it was just too tempting. Please, forget that happened.'

Lilah glowered at him. That was easy for him to say. He probably went round kissing women all the time so one more wouldn't make a difference. In fact, she knew from experience that he did. But it was different for her. That had only been her second kiss and this was not how she'd imagined it. Nor would she be able to forget it. How could she?

Disappointment flooded her. So this was what she'd condemned herself to with her actions – being kissed by men who didn't mean anything by it, who thought her fair game. She crossed her arms over her chest, belatedly realising that her shift may be somewhat see-through, and waited to see what he'd do next.

'Really, I apologise,' he said, getting off the bed. He retrieved his Hessian boots and pulled them on with some difficulty. "I'll go and order us some breakfast and I won't return until you're ready to come downstairs.'

'Isn't it a bit early?' She glanced at the window which showed that dawn had only just broken.

'The sooner we leave the better.' He turned serious again. 'We may have beaten Braithwaite and his cronies last night, but there's no guarantee they won't try and find us to exact revenge, bringing more of their nasty friends. We shouldn't tarry.'

'Very well. I'll be ready in a trice.'

The sooner they left this bedroom, the better it would be, in her opinion.

Although a tiny voice inside her said that wasn't quite true. If he'd kissed her again, she might have been very tempted to stay.

Hamish wanted to go and dunk his head in the horses' water trough in the courtyard to shock some sense into himself. What on earth had come over him? He still didn't even know if he could trust Delilah, and yet he'd kissed her. What an imbecile.

But he couldn't stop himself from remembering

the feel of her luscious mouth against his. Seemingly innocent, yet tempting beyond belief. He'd wanted to do it again. Pull her into his arms and hold her close. Stroke her velvet skin and bury his fingers in her lovely hair ...

No. What was he thinking? He didn't know her, not really, and he was sure she hadn't shown her true colours yet. Yes, she'd helped him the night before, but that could have been sheer self-preservation. And she could still be playing a deep game. He wouldn't be deceived by another Risden chit. Touching her in any way would be a grave mistake and he had no intention of doing it again. From now on, he'd insist on separate rooms or sleep in the stables if necessary. He simply couldn't share with her.

That way lay danger.

Chapter Five

'We need to make up some sort of story to account for the fact that I've hired you,' Hamish said as they approached the Scottish border. 'Would you mind remaining Mrs Robarts?'

'Pretend I'm a widow, you mean?'

'Exactly.' He liked the way she caught on immediately and came straight to the point. 'I could say that you'd only just married a friend of mine who then got himself killed in the Peninsular war. It happens and you wouldn't be the first. I hear the ladies find it difficult to resist a man in a uniform and you are young and impressionable.'

'I am not!'

Hamish smiled at the outrage in her voice. No, he doubted she'd have fallen for a penniless soldier. She had more sense than that, as he was discovering. 'For the purposes of our little charade I need you to be,' he insisted. 'Who's to know that it's not the truth, except me?'

'Very well. I'm not sure they'll believe this tale anyway, but it's worth a try.'

'It will be up to you to convince them and you'll have to pretend to be grieving. The black gowns should help. But either way, they will have no choice but to accept you as I'm the one who has appointed you housekeeper.'

Still, he knew the other servants could make life difficult for her in ways he couldn't control and he wouldn't always be there to protect her. He had other estates to look after and also various business interests.

But somehow he felt certain Delilah could hold her own.

He hoped he wasn't wrong.

Just north of Carlisle, Lilah's horse began to limp and they were forced to stop at the nearest inn.

'Oh dear, what are we to do now?' Lilah stroked the horse who seemed reassured by her mistress's touch and allowed Hamish to examine the leg and hoof.

'No visible damage so he must just have overdone it. I think the best thing will be if we hire a carriage and tie our horses to the back. We've obviously ridden them too hard but I'm sure yours can cope as long as there's no weight on his back.'

'Won't that be expensive though? And how will you get the carriage back here?'

Hamish looked up, an expression of surprise crossing his features. 'You're worried about the cost? I'm not going to make you pay for it, you know. It could just as well have been my horse who went lame.'

Lilah felt her cheeks heat up. 'Well, no, I didn't think you would, but I'm causing you unnecessary expense and I don't want to be a burden. You've already been very kind in bringing me north personally and ... er, taken care of me.'

She didn't want to mention the fact that she was grateful he hadn't forced himself on her. There was no denying the fact that she'd put herself in this situation and could have been considered fair game, a single woman travelling un-chaperoned with a man. The situation was indecent, but he had shown her nothing but respect ... Well, apart from one kiss.

She didn't want to think about that.

He smiled and shook his head. 'Don't give it a moment's thought. I believe you've saved me from far greater expenditure. Somehow I don't think your sister would have been a cheap wife.'

Lilah had to agree with that.

They set off again in a hired carriage, with a coachman who alleged he knew the way. 'I come from Inveraray so I know me way around,' he told them, which seemed good enough for Hamish.

'We'll be passing Gretna Green soon,' Hamish told her halfway through the afternoon.

Lilah stared out the window and tried to quash the sudden desolation that swept through her. How different – how exciting – it would have been if they were an eloping couple, on their way to Gretna. If Hamish had ever asked her to follow him there, she would have jumped at the chance. She didn't give a fig for society weddings or any of the other trappings Deborah had considered so important. She just wanted to be with the man she loved.

But that would never happen now. Who would want her?

And she'd never want anyone other than Hamish.

The first time she'd seen him across a crowded ballroom she had known he was the one. It seemed ridiculously clichéd, falling in love at first sight, but once she set eyes on him, every other man in the room faded into the background as though they didn't exist. It wasn't just his looks – although no one could deny he was extraordinarily handsome – but the way he carried himself, the good humour that sparkled in his sapphire eyes, his devastating smile, his carefree laughter. She couldn't explain it, even to herself, but she was drawn to him without having exchanged so much as a word.

Naturally, his first inclination upon being introduced to the Risden family was to ask Deborah to dance. Lilah had attended a few balls and parties by then and was becoming accustomed to being invisible, unless Deborah was on the dance floor. Second best, the quiet one, the sensible one – no one said those things out loud, but she could tell that's what they thought. And she couldn't deny it was true.

It only hurt where Hamish was concerned.

Deborah had a sparkle, a vivacity and zest for life that Lilah simply couldn't compete with. She had resigned herself to waiting to find a husband once Deborah was safely married off. It had seemed the only way.

But then she'd seen Hamish and despite everything, a girl could dream …

Hamish noticed that Lilah went very quiet when he mentioned Gretna Green. He'd done it deliberately, as a sort of test. He wanted to see what she'd do or say. If she was scheming to make him marry her after all, here was her chance. Perhaps she thought she'd fooled him into thinking her entirely unlike her sister by now and susceptible to her undoubted charms. She could plead with him to save her reputation, cry a little – most men had a hard time withstanding tears after all – and appeal to his gentlemanly nature.

She didn't say a word.

Instead she began a conversation about Lord Byron and his latest poem, asking if he'd read it and what he thought. Hamish could only surmise she truly didn't want to marry him or her motives had been as altruistic as she'd claimed. Otherwise, why would she let such a chance go by?

He wondered if she was in love with someone else. Someone who'd rejected her? Perhaps that was why she didn't care about her reputation. If she had no intention of marrying anyone, it made sense for her to throw caution to the wind.

Still, he had a hard time believing this.

Damn it all, why couldn't he just trust her? But he was afraid of being made to look a fool again.

He racked his brains, trying to remember if he'd heard any gossip about her in London, but nothing came to mind. If anything, the talk had all been of Deborah and her undoubted beauty. Then again, he'd never been one to listen to idle tattle, especially not about debutantes. He rarely gave them a thought, preferring to spend time with his friends, riding, racing his phaeton, gambling – although never to excess, he wasn't stupid – and flirting with women. He always chose mature ones who knew the rules of the game and didn't expect a ring on their finger. A carefree, easy life; his only obligations to look after his estates, something he enjoyed in any case.

That evening he'd apparently danced with Delilah, what had they talked about? He recalled thinking her unusually subdued, but with a dry wit that had been lacking before. More sensible, less frivolous, almost shy. Was that Lilah's true nature? He was beginning to believe it was.

He had to stop connecting her with Deborah in his

mind. Lilah was her own person, one he was beginning to like more than he wanted to admit.

Just northeast of Dumfries, they heard yelling and gun shots and the carriage came to an abrupt halt, throwing them both forward onto the opposite seat.

'What the ...? Damnation!' Hamish bit back further swear words and righted himself, before helping Lilah back onto the seat. 'Are you hurt?'

'No, I'm fine, but what's going on?'

Hamish pulled the window down to see and was annoyed to find two highwaymen blocking their way. In broad daylight? They must be desperate, although to be fair, this was a rather desolate stretch of road with dense forest on either side.

'Stand and deliver!' they shouted.

Hamish ducked back inside and pulled up the window again. 'Shield me for a moment,' he hissed at Lilah, while rooting around in his saddle bags which were on the floor next to him. He found the pair of pistols he always travelled with and started to load them at record speed.

Lilah glanced back at him. 'What are you planning to do?' she whispered. 'Are you going to kill them?'

'No, not if I can help it. I'll just try to wing them. They'll make us get out of the coach any moment now. Do you think you could try to create a small diversion so that one of them is only paying attention to you? Pretend to faint or something.'

'Very well.'

He saw Lilah pull something out of her own saddle bags and hide it under her skirt. 'What are you—?' he started to say, but was cut off by one of the highwaymen who yanked the door open and stuck his pistol in through the opening.

'Come outside, now, the pair of ye. And don't try nothin' clever.'

Lilah, who was nearest the door, exited first. Hamish saw her hold her head high and glare at the highwayman who'd retreated a few steps. Hamish followed and stood close to her. 'What do you want?'

'What do yer think? Yer valuables, o'course.' Even though they couldn't see the man's mouth under the scarf tied round the lower half of his face, the sneer in his voice was clear. Hamish felt fury bubble up inside him.

'We didn't bring much. We had to leave home in a rush.' He put his hand in his pocket and took out a few coins. 'This is all we have left.'

The man stepped forward a step and snarled, 'Do yer think I was born yesterday?' He slapped Hamish's hand, scattering the measly coins across the ground.

Hamish nudged Delilah, hoping she could create a believable diversion, a fainting fit or some such thing. To his surprise, she drew out her riding crop from the folds of her skirt and struck the man hard across one cheek. He let out a yell of pain and stumbled backwards. Hamish took his chance and brought out one of the pistols, which he'd shoved down the back of his breeches. Taking aim, he quickly fired at the other highwayman, who was sitting on horseback nearby and who'd had his musket trained on the coachman and therefore wasn't paying proper attention to Hamish. The man was hit in the leg and screamed, letting off his musket by mistake. The shot whizzed by but fortunately only hit a tree. The man's horse was so spooked, however, he took off with the screaming man and disappeared down the track.

Hamish didn't waste time watching. As soon as he'd shot the first highwayman, he threw himself at the second one, grabbing the hand that held the pistol and forcing the wrist back until it nearly snapped. The man howled in agony and the pistol clattered to the ground. Delilah swiftly picked it up and aimed it at the man's temple.

'Stand still or I'll shoot,' she threatened. 'And don't think I can't do it just because I'm a female. I assure you I'm perfectly capable of pulling the trigger.'

Hamish almost smiled. She had him convinced, never mind the highwayman, who'd frozen the instant he felt the pistol's nozzle against his head. Hamish pulled off his neck cloth and used it to tie the man's hands behind his back, then he pushed him into the carriage and onto the floor. 'Don't move,' he commanded.

Hamish took the pistol from Lilah and noticed that she was shaking, but otherwise composed. He was seriously impressed and his admiration for her rose another notch. She was quite something, this woman.

'Well done,' he whispered, and without thinking he wrapped his arms around her and pulled her tight to his chest. The relief of seeing her unhurt was much greater than he would have imagined and he realised that he cared about her. 'Are you all right?' he asked, his voice gruff with emotion which he couldn't quite hide.

'Yes, thank you.' Her words were muffled against his coat and for a moment he felt her arms go round him, squeezing hard as if she too was glad he wasn't harmed. In the next instant she pushed against his chest with her hands and took a step back. She stared at the ground, as if embarrassed, and he saw her take a deep breath. 'Well done yourself. You really are a good shot, unless that was a lucky hit?' She looked up and tried to smile and he admired her bravado.

'Trust me, that was not down to luck.' He grinned back. 'I go to Manton's often to practise.'

And right now he was very glad he had. If anything had happened to her … He didn't want to think about that. He held out a hand to help her to climb back into the conveyance. 'We'd better be on our way in case there are others of his ilk.' He indicated the man lying prone on the floor of the carriage.

After Hamish had checked to make sure the coachman was unharmed, and asked him to stop at the nearest inn so they could hand the thief over to the authorities, they continued their journey but it was a long while before Hamish's heartbeat returned to normal.

'I don't understand why we had to go gallivanting off to London in such a rush. I'd have thought you'd not want to show your face here for a while. Goodness knows I don't! And your Papa said you were to stay in your room, so he won't be best pleased when he comes home to find us both gone.'

Lady Risden had been grumbling all the way to the capital and Deborah was heartily sick of listening to her mother, but for once she held her tongue. She needed to find out where Lilah had gone and she couldn't go to London on her own. It simply wasn't done.

'Papa will believe the note you left him. You did say we had to visit Aunt Sarah because she's unwell, didn't you?' When Lady Risden nodded, Deborah continued, 'There you are then. He can't object to that. And it's not as if we're here to see anyone, I told you. I just think it's our duty to fetch Lilah back. Surely you don't want to leave her to fend for herself in this place?'

Her mother threw her a suspicious glance which was understandable since Deborah had never before expressed any concern for her sister's welfare. 'Well, no but ...'

'I don't deny I'm still angry with her, but if I'm to prove to everyone that I didn't do anything wrong, I'll need her to publicly apologise and take back what she said. That's the only way, don't you see?' Deborah didn't add that once she'd forced Lilah to retract all her statements and swear they were lies entirely made up by her out of jealousy, she'd be adding her own punishments to those no doubt meted out by their father. For now, she had to keep her mother on her side.

Lady Risden sighed. 'I suppose you're right. The silly chit will definitely have to apologise. You're sure that—?'

'Yes, Mama. We've been over this a hundred times already – I did *not* put laudanum in Lord Blackwood's tea.'

'Well, there was that time when you put great-uncle Hector to sleep for an entire day.' Lady Risden frowned at the memory. 'He was furious afterwards.'

'It was a childish prank, years ago.' Deborah giggled. 'He did look funny, didn't he? Snoring away and no one could lift him to get him to bed, he was so fat.'

On a more serious note, the incident had been useful in showing Deborah the wisdom of a smaller dose of the sleeping draught, but she didn't mention that now.

'*And* you put salt in the sugar bowl, annoying my sister Lavinia no end. Not to mention that time you …

'For heaven's sake, Mama, must we reminisce about every one of my little misdemeanours? They have no bearing on this matter and why would I need to use such methods on the earl? I was the most sought-after catch on the marriage mart. A diamond of the first water – Lord Blackwood said so himself.' Even though that hadn't meant he wanted to marry her.

Deborah had managed to persuade her mother that Lilah had made up the whole thing. And unlike her husband, Lady Risden believed it. She'd always had a soft spot for Deborah and knew her daughter had had numerous suitors, which made the lie more convincing. The fact that Lord Blackwood had been the only man not to succumb to Deborah's wiles in the usual way was something no one needed to know.

'So what are you going to do?'

'Oh, don't worry, I'll think of something.' In fact, Deborah had several plans and had put them in motion as soon as they'd arrived in London. First of all she'd hired someone to keep watch on Lord Blackwood's town house and report back any comings and goings. Then she'd sent out several of the servants to check with various employment agencies if anyone fitting Lilah's description had turned up recently.

One way or another, she'd find her sister. And when she did, Lilah would be very sorry.

Chapter Six

'Welcome to Coille Dubh.'

Lilah's horse had recovered sufficiently for her to ride the final stretch to their destination, which was just as well since the roads were very poor. Hamish had now reined in his stallion on a hill at the entrance to a small glen, and Lilah looked down at a sparkling loch and a settlement next to its shore. At the centre was a small stone keep with a square tower in one corner. The grey stone looked as old as the hills around it and seemed almost to be a part of the landscape.

So this was his Scottish home. It was much more modest than she'd expected, but that pleased her. It confirmed her opinion that Hamish was no vain peacock whose properties were bought just for showing off with. No, this was a place to be comfortable in, she could feel it. A real home.

Along the road leading to this building were other dwellings with thatched roofs. Smoke drifted out of the top of them so that they looked as though they were smouldering. It was a charming and peaceful sight, the smell of the wood smoke teasing her nostrils.

'Coille Dubh? Is that the name of the keep or the whole valley?'

'It's called a glen here, the valley that is, and yes, it's the name of the entire estate which stretches into several more glens in that direction.' He pointed away from them. 'It means "black forest", hence the name

Blackwood, which my ancestors adopted for their English holdings as well.'

Lilah knew he had a substantial amount of English acres somewhere in Wiltshire, as well as other smaller estates. Deborah had gone on at great length about how she would no doubt have to have the entire house redecorated, since his lordship's ancestors probably had no taste whatsoever. 'It will be such fun, and as he's rich as Croesus, I'm sure he won't mind the expense.'

Lilah wasn't as certain, but hadn't said a word.

'It's beautiful,' she said now, taking in the stark grandeur of their surroundings. 'But I can't see a forest anywhere.' In fact, since they had entered the Highlands, the hillsides seemed mostly bare, apart from the heather, and although there were trees lower down, they didn't constitute a forest to her mind.

Hamish laughed. 'No, not now, but I think there may have been one here a long time ago. Or so I've been told.' He turned serious again. 'Are you ready?'

Lilah nodded and gripped the reins tighter. Truth to tell, she was feeling very nervous. She doubted Hamish's other servants would welcome her with open arms despite their made up story. Not only was she a newcomer – and an English one at that – but she was extremely young to be put in such a position of authority, widow or not. It would have been a different matter if she'd been his wife ... She stifled the thought and swallowed hard. He hadn't made that offer again so now she had to cope with the consequences of her own rash actions.

Well, she didn't regret what she'd done. She raised her chin a notch. And she'd show everyone here that she could run a household, despite her tender age. With determination stiffening her backbone, she followed Hamish down the path.

'Good afternoon, Findlay, I trust you are well?'

Hamish handed his hat and riding gloves to his Scottish butler, who'd been waiting on the steps up to the keep. No doubt someone had spotted the approaching riders and warned him, as he hid his surprise at this visit with admirable *sangfroid*.

'Very well, thank you, my lord. We were not expecting you today, but I'm sure Cook will prepare some refreshments immediately.' Findlay glanced at Delilah. 'I'll have a guest room prepared for the, er, young lady.'

'That won't be necessary. This is Mrs Robarts and she'll be occupying the housekeeper's room. She's to take on Mrs McDuff's role with immediate effect.'

Findlay's eyes widened for a moment, before he resumed his passive expression. 'I see. Very well, I'll have that made ready instead then.' He bowed to Delilah. 'Welcome to Coille Dubh, Mrs Robarts.'

'Thank you, Mr Findlay. I look forward to working with you.'

Hamish noticed that she remembered to address the butler as 'Mr' and not just by his surname the way she would normally have done. As housekeeper, Findlay was more or less her equal in the hierarchy of servants. Hamish couldn't help but admire Delilah's poise and the fact that she wasn't letting her nerves show. He was sure she must be feeling intimidated, as would anyone in her position, but she smiled calmly at Findlay and

Hamish saw the old butler's expression relax a tiny bit. *So she's begun to charm him already,* he thought. *Good.* With Findlay as her ally, her job would be that much easier.

'Mrs Robarts and I will await refreshments here,' he said. 'We need to discuss her duties in any case and that will give you time to prepare our rooms.'

'Very good, my lord.' Findlay hesitated. 'Is your valet arriving later today?'

Hamish frowned. 'Is he not here yet? He was supposed to have arrived before us.' He didn't want to admit that he had no idea where the valet might be, so he added, 'Perhaps he's met with some accident.' He shrugged. 'It's a damned nuisance – begging your pardon Mrs Robarts – you'll have to assign someone else to help me in the meantime, Findlay.'

'Yes, of course, my lord.'

'Right then, please take a seat over here, Mrs Robarts. Let us discuss your employment in more detail.'

Lilah looked around her surreptitiously as she followed Hamish over to a fireplace at one end of the room. They had gone up a set of outside stairs and come straight into what looked like a great medieval hall, complete with thick stone walls and huge roof beams. On the walls were colourful hangings and various hunting trophies, as well as some old weapons. The floor was covered in rugs that looked in need of a good beating and she noticed that some of the furniture could do with dusting. In fact, the whole room had an air of neglect and the spiders had obviously been allowed to proliferate in peace. That would have to change.

It looked like she had her work cut out for the foreseeable future, but she didn't mind. She would enjoy setting everything to rights. Hamish had told her the house had been without Mrs McDuff for nigh on two months now, so it was definitely time for someone to take up the reins of authority.

'How many rooms do you have here?' she ventured to ask.

'Oh, about a dozen bed chambers, this hall, a dining room, small sitting room and my study. Then there are the kitchens and servants' quarters, of course, but it's not what you'd call a huge mansion. Are you disappointed?'

He was looking at her with his head to one side, as if assessing her reaction to his home. She smiled.

'No, not at all, it's charming. And if it's not massive it will be so much easier for me to manage everything.'

'Just so.' She thought she saw a glimmer of pleasure in his eyes at the fact that she liked Coille Dubh, but he didn't say anything else on the subject.

'Now, about your salary,' he began instead. 'I shall pay you the going rate, of course, but as you may be a bit low on funds, I'll advance you the first quarter's wages immediately, agreed?'

Lilah nodded. 'Thank you, that would be very kind.' She didn't tell him about the jewels she'd brought in case of emergencies. If she could survive on her salary, and perhaps even save some more, so much the better. One day she might even be able to live independently, renting a small cottage somewhere. That would have to be her goal now.

'You may find there is some slight resistance to your

authority at first,' Hamish was saying. 'Can you handle that? I won't be able to stay for very long this time.'

'Yes, of course. As I told you, I'm used to running a household. Mama has been poorly for the last few years and Deborah never took an interest in such things, so it fell to me to sort everything out.' Her chin came up again. 'I know what I'm doing.'

He smiled and held up his hands, as if surrendering. 'I believe you, it's just ...' His eyes flickered over her for a brief moment, before coming to rest on her face once more. 'You are rather young and, uhm, lovely, you know. There will undoubtedly be those who assume that I have employed you for, shall we say, not altogether altruistic reasons.'

Lilah felt her cheeks flame, even though she already knew this. As for the fact that he considered her 'lovely' ... she wouldn't think about that. After all, he must have thought the same about Deborah but it didn't mean he wanted to marry her. She concentrated on the here and now. 'Well, we will just have to show them they're wrong. And I doubt you'll spend much time in my company. If you don't mind me asking, how many months a year do you reside here? And will I be arranging any house parties?'

'I usually spend at least two or three months here, from August onwards, and also a month or two in spring. And yes, I daresay I'll invite some guests, but don't worry, I will give you plenty of notice.'

'Thank you.'

Their refreshments arrived, served by Findlay himself, and the conversation dwindled. Lilah almost felt as if an invisible barrier had gone up between them. Where before they had been equals, now she was Hamish's servant and no longer someone he could hold a personal conversation with. From now on he'd merely be giving her orders. And she had to remember her place. She was a housekeeper and had to live a life of servitude. It was a lowering thought, but at least she didn't have to suffer Deborah and her selfish antics any longer. That was definitely a silver lining.

'I'm sorry I can't invite you to eat your meals with me.' Hamish was frowning, as if he'd only just realised this. 'But it would look dashed suspicious, don't you think?'

'Of course, I understand.'

Lilah didn't mind eating on her own and followed Findlay to her room as soon as it was ready. They walked along dark, stone-walled corridors and up and down odd staircases. Hamish's Scottish keep seemed to have been built in a rather haphazard manner, or perhaps it had been added to over time. Lilah knew she'd soon get her bearings, but for now she was glad to have the butler as her guide.

They didn't see another soul along the way. It was as if everyone was staying out of sight and Lilah had the uncomfortable feeling of being watched by eyes she couldn't see. But she held her head high and ignored it. She'd meet the rest of the household soon enough, and if they'd prefer it to be the following day, that suited her very well.

She needed to gather her strength and courage first anyway.

Lilah was up at the crack of dawn the following day, having slept surprisingly well in her new room. By her previous standards, it was tiny, but it had everything she needed – a comfortable bed, wash stand, wardrobe, chair and small fireplace – and it was hers alone. Her window, which had a deep embrasure that showed clearly how thick the house's outer walls were, had amazing views along the loch and cushions to sit on. The water was beautifully calm today and mirrored the majestic hills along its sides. She decided this was definitely not a bad place to live.

'Good morning. I trust you all slept well?'

She swept into the kitchen, dressed in her black woollen dress, with the housekeeper's keys in her pocket. Findlay had handed them over the previous evening after serving her supper on a tray in her room.

'Cook knows what they're all for. She's kept them since Mrs McDuff's passing,' he'd told her, but from his expression she gathered that Cook may not wish to share her knowledge.

Well, they'd just see about that.

At her greeting, four pairs of more or less hostile eyes looked up from whatever tasks they were performing and all activity in the kitchen stopped for a moment as everyone assessed her. Lilah pretended she hadn't noticed anything out of the ordinary and added, 'I'm Mrs Robarts, the new housekeeper hired by Lord Blackwood, as I'm sure Mr Findlay has informed you, and I hope we shall all work well together. May I know your names, please?'

Findlay wasn't there to introduce her, which was a touch annoying, but then the butler had probably been taken by surprise by her arrival and simply forgotten about her this morning. Or he didn't want to have to act as mediator. She deliberately mentioned the fact that it was his lordship who had appointed her, just to make sure this fact was emphasised. It didn't seem to be making much difference though as no one said anything at first.

The older woman standing by a huge range finally wiped her hands on her apron and came forward slowly. 'I'm Mrs Kendrick, the cook,' she said, then indicated two younger women, one of whom looked to be in her mid-twenties while the other was much younger. 'This is Moira.' She pointed at the older maid. 'And that's Shona. They help with whatever is needed.'

Lilah received a glare from Moira, a pretty redhead with shiny curls barely contained under her cap. She seemed even more hostile than the others and Lilah wondered why, but didn't have time to ponder this at the moment.

Mrs Kendrick was introducing a young man about the same age as Lilah. 'And here's Jameson, footman normally, but acting as valet to his lordship for now.'

Lilah nodded to them. 'Pleased to meet you all.' She looked to the cook, as she was obviously the person in charge at the moment. 'Is there anyone else employed here, apart from Mr Findlay?'

Mrs Kendrick shook her head. 'Not unless you count the steward, Mr Armstrong, and the grooms and gardener.'

'I see. Well, as there isn't an abundance of staff, I assume we all pitch in where necessary?' Mrs Kendrick nodded reluctantly, as though she wasn't sure where Lilah's question was leading.

'I'm mostly busy with the cooking though,' the

71

woman muttered, presumably in case Lilah had any thoughts of putting her to work elsewhere in the house.

'Of course.' Lilah smiled to show she wouldn't dream of taking the cook away from this task. 'I'd be happy to help prepare breakfast, then I wondered if perhaps you'd have time to show me around and tell me how things are done here? I realise I have a lot to learn about this place and although I'm used to running an English estate, no doubt there are differences.'

She hoped that by not storming in and imposing her own ways immediately, she could win the trust of the servants, even though she was nominally in command of them all. Mrs Kendrick looked surprised, but slightly mollified and visibly relaxed her stance. 'Aye, I reckon I could do that.'

'Thank you. What would you have me do now then?'

'I'm sure we can manage. Always have done before.'

'I don't doubt it, but I thought perhaps an extra pair of hands would help. Is that porridge you're making?' Lilah had no intention of running away. The sooner these people learned that, the better. She was here to stay whether they liked it or not.

'That it is. His lordship insists on it whenever he's here. Good plain Scottish fare.' This was uttered almost as a challenge, as if Lilah would object. She hid a smile. She'd never been spoiled, despite her privileged upbringing, and ate whatever was put in front of her.

'Excellent, porridge is my favourite.' Lilah wasn't lying, she really did like it, although some bread and butter with a dish of tea wouldn't go amiss as well. Luckily, the cook soon showed her that Lord

Blackwood also wanted those, along with cold meats and scrambled eggs.

'He has a large appetite of a morning,' Mrs Kendrick murmured, but Lilah got the impression this pleased the woman as it showed that her employer appreciated her cooking skills. 'Here, you can stir if you wish. Just keep the porridge from sticking to the pot while I see to the eggs.'

Lilah could do that, even if most housekeepers wouldn't. If it helped earn Mrs Kendrick's trust, so be it.

Chapter Seven

Hamish was already up and dressed when Jameson brought his shaving water. In fact, he'd been awake for ages wondering if he'd done the right thing in bringing Delilah here. She was so young and inexperienced, how would she cope? But what else could he have done? And she had faced down both bullies and highwaymen with huge courage so surely she could cope with a gaggle of servants?

'My lord! You … you didn't ring for me.' Jameson looked startled to see that his master had obviously coped without him.

'I'm perfectly capable of dressing myself,' Hamish said, then hastened to add, 'and I was sure you'd have plenty of other chores this morning so I didn't want to add to your workload,' when he saw the young servant's chagrined expression and realised the man would take it as an insult that he didn't want his services.

'Oh, I see.' Jameson put the jug of hot water down. 'Would you like me to help you with shaving?'

'Are you good at it?' Hamish smiled to show that he didn't mean any offence.

'Yes, Mr Findlay's been training me himself, so he has.'

'Well, in that case, yes please.'

Hamish would normally do it himself but he could see the young man was eager to show off his skills. No doubt he hoped for a promotion eventually and Hamish always encouraged his staff to learn new skills and try to better themselves. He didn't believe in keeping them down-trodden and he was glad Findlay was following his orders in this respect.

'How is the new housekeeper settling in?' he asked casually, as if he didn't really care about the answer, which was far from the truth. He'd thought of nothing else since he woke up.

Damnation. She was just a woman and one who'd willingly created a scandal. Yes, it had been for his benefit, but he still wasn't convinced that was all there was to it. Surely no one was that self-sacrificing and good? Although, truth to tell, even he was beginning to believe he was over-thinking this. Why could he not just accept what he was seeing? Delilah was exactly the person she seemed to be.

'She's … ah, cookin' porridge,' Jameson replied, while stirring the shaving soap into a lather.

'What?' Hamish, who had leaned back in his chair, sat up straight again. 'Is Cook ill?'

'Erm, no. Mrs Robarts is just helpin' like. I think she said somethin' about us all workin' together?'

'Ah, right. Well, good.' Hamish relaxed again as understanding dawned. Delilah was doing things in her own, gentle way. She'd obviously realised that acting like a general on manoeuvres wouldn't get her anywhere so she was trying the softer approach. He hoped it would work.

Perhaps he'd send for her later just to make sure.

'Mrs Robarts, may I introduce Mr Armstrong, my steward?'

Lilah had been called to Lord Blackwood's study as

soon as she'd finished the tour of the house with Mrs Kendrick, which had gone better than she'd expected. When she commiserated with the cook about having to take on the duties of housekeeper, as well as her own tasks, and assured her she'd listen to her advice on all things – at least to begin with – Mrs Kendrick appeared much relieved and definitely friendlier. As for the other servants, Lilah hoped they'd follow the cook's lead.

'How do you do?' She curtseyed politely now to an older man with spectacles perched on his rather prominent nose.

'Pleased to meet you, Miss … er, Mrs Robarts.'

She saw Hamish send the man a scowl but she didn't blame him for his mistake. Most people would assume her to be unmarried, but they'd just have to get used to thinking her a widow. It was perfectly possible after all, even if it wasn't true.

'You will of course be in charge of the household accounts,' Hamish was saying, 'but please confer with Armstrong at the end of each week. He deals with all the tradesmen's bills and so on and pays the staff's wages.'

'Very well. That shouldn't be a problem.' She smiled at Mr Armstrong who looked like a gentle soul and he seemed relieved at her friendliness. 'I assure you I've done accounts before and I'll endeavour to add up correctly.'

'Good, good.' He beamed at her and nodded.

'That will be all then, thank you, Armstrong. I'll sign those letters later.' Hamish nodded dismissal at his steward, who bowed himself out of the room. 'Now, how would you like a walk outside, Del— I mean, Mrs Robarts?'

'Is that a good idea? I should be working, not spending time with you, my lord.' Lilah had been very tempted to just say yes. It was such a relief to be with someone she didn't have to play-act in front of, if only for a short while. She ignored the little voice inside which said she simply wanted to spend time with Hamish while she still could. Soon he'd be gone.

'I've told Armstrong I'm going to show you round the garden and village. Perfectly proper,' Hamish said.

'If you're sure, then yes please. I'll just fetch my bonnet and shawl.' Even though it was May, the weather was still chilly up here in the north.

After a walk along the road that constituted the village and a tour of the grounds, they strolled down a path in a walled garden, where a gardener laboured over some vegetable beds. Hamish introduced her briefly, then swept her along towards the loch. 'I wanted to show you the view from down here,' he told her. 'What do you think?' He swept a hand out to indicate more or less the same sight as the one she'd seen from her window that morning, only here it seemed closer and even more majestic. A breeze had stirred up little waves now, but the loch was no less beautiful for that.

'I love it,' Lilah said simply. 'You have a beautiful home, my lord.'

'I'm glad you like it. This is the place where I feel most at peace and I sometimes wonder ... but no, you don't want to hear about that.' He looked away as though he was embarrassed.

Lilah was intrigued. He'd always seemed so confident to her, but perhaps there was another side to him? 'No, tell me. Please. I'd like to know,' she said.

'Really? You'll think me fanciful, but very well. When I'm here, I feel as though all my ancestors are watching over me, helping me. Silly really, but there it is. And I wish I could spend all my time here, rather than gallivanting up and down the country. But owning estates brings obligations, unfortunately, and I have to make sure they're all run properly. There's no one else as I have no siblings or close relatives.' He shrugged. 'So there you have it. The strange fancies of Lord Blackwood.'

Lilah put a hand on his arm and squeezed. 'Not strange at all. I could well believe there are spirits here, watching over you. It's a magical place.'

She didn't add that he was a good man for caring about his estates. Despite his reputation as a rake there was obviously a much more serious part of him, one he never showed the *ton*. Lilah was pleased to discover this as it made her even more sure that she'd done the right thing in saving him from Deborah. He deserved better.

He placed his hand on top of hers, his fingers warm against her smaller ones. 'Thank you. I will ask them to watch over you too. You are part of this place now as well.'

Lilah looked up towards the keep and thought she saw a flash of red hair duck away from one of the windows. Moira? She hoped not. She quickly disentangled her hand from under Hamish's even though she very much wanted to cling onto it, and turned away. 'That's very kind,' she murmured. 'And now I'd better get back to earning that place. Thank you for the tour.'

Hamish travelled back to London the following day

and Lilah felt as though he left a huge void behind him. She hadn't realised how much she'd come to rely on his company, but she told herself she didn't need him. There was work to do and she was determined to prove herself worthy of her position.

Coming down the steps to the kitchen, she faltered when she heard herself being discussed, albeit in low voices.

'She's a hussy, I tell ye, Mrs Kendrick. Saw it with me own eyes, I did. It's as plain as day, she's warmed his bed and now he's tirin' of her so he's foisted her on us. She's no better than she should be.' Moira's not so dulcet tones. Lilah should have guessed but she was startled by the vitriol in the woman's voice. Was she jealous? The cook's reply seemed to confirm this.

'That's the pot calling the kettle black, if ever I heard it,' Mrs Kendrick murmured. 'Weren't you setting your cap at his lordship last time he was here? You're just miffed he didn't accept your invitation.'

'I'm not!'

'Well, it makes no odds, does it, what she is? As long as she performs her duties as housekeeper.'

'Of course it does! Why should we take orders from the likes of her?' Moira hissed.

'Because that's what you're paid to do,' the older woman shot back.

Before they could continue their conversation, Lilah cleared her throat loudly to alert them to her imminent arrival. She walked into the kitchen with a cheery 'Good morning,' then continued, 'It's time for a spring clean, wouldn't you say, Mrs Kendrick?' She didn't wait for the cook to object. 'May I borrow Moira and Shona, please? And perhaps you could be so kind as to heat up some water? We'll need lots of it.'

Shona eagerly left off peeling vegetables, a boring and seemingly never-ending task, while Moira tried to protest that she was busy. 'Rubbish,' Mrs Kendrick told her with a stern look. 'You've no more to do than Shona.'

Both maids seemed startled when Lilah joined in with the cleaning, but she'd never been one for watching while others worked. 'Are ye sure ye want to be doin' this, Mrs Robarts?' Shona ventured to ask.

Lilah smiled at her. 'Of course. It'll be done much faster with three pairs of hands, don't you think?'

And with Lilah doing part of the work herself, there was no excuse for Moira not to do her bit. Lilah hid a smile. The woman was definitely jealous, having thought she'd seen something going on between Lilah and his lordship. She was glad he hadn't taken advantage of Moira during other visits, although it was none of her business – or so she told herself. For now, Moira was under Lilah's command and if she wanted to keep her job, she'd have to work for it.

'I have some news for you at last, Miss. He's back.'

Deborah was standing at the back of the hall near the door to the servants' quarters and the footman who'd delivered this momentous news was talking in a hushed whisper.

'Oh, good. Where had he come from, did you find out?'

'Indeed I did.' The footman smiled. 'I had a word with the coachman's assistant, a young lad who'd never been to London before by the look of it. He was looking round with eyes as big as guineas and—'

'Yes, yes, but what did he say?' Deborah didn't pay the man to bring her gossip about Lord Blackwood's servants. She only wanted to know about the man himself.

'Oh, yes, right. They'd come from Scotland. His lordship has an estate there and according to the lad he'd brought them a new housekeeper.'

'Really?' Deborah couldn't believe her luck. Housekeeper – now that sounded just like the ideal position for Lilah. 'Young? Old? Did he say anything about her?'

'Oh, definitely young. He seemed rather taken with her, said she was a stunner.'

'I see.' That was less welcome news. Deborah didn't consider her sister as beautiful as herself, despite the fact that they were identical twins. She had always been the one to shine.

It had to be Delilah though. The coincidence was too great otherwise. Had her twin blackmailed his lordship into hiring her? It was entirely possible. What other choice had she had after all? No one would hire someone so young, especially without references. And Deborah doubted Lord Blackwood would have offered marriage, no matter how grateful he was to get out of matrimony with herself. That thought stung – he should have been pleased to have her.

'You are sure about this?' she asked the footman.

'Absolutely, Miss. The lad was as green as they come, I don't think he'd know how to lie.'

'Excellent, thank you. Please continue to keep an eye

out and let me know where his lordship goes next.'
She gave the footman his remuneration, paying him
handsomely to keep him on side, then wandered into
the morning room, her head in a whirl. She had plans
to make and whereas before these had been vague, now
that she knew where to find her sister they could be
shaped into something concrete.

It was all falling into place very neatly.

Chapter Eight

Two weeks after Lord Blackwood's departure the entire house was as clean and fragrant as it could possibly be. Woodwork and furniture had been polished, carpets beaten, shelves dusted, hangings and curtains washed or aired. There wasn't a corner of the keep where any self-respecting spider would want to stay and Lilah felt very satisfied with what she had achieved so far.

'We mustn't let it get out of hand from now on,' she told the others. 'And I'm not blaming you, Mrs Kendrick, I know you had your own chores to see to so it was too much to ask that you should keep on top of the cleaning as well. From now on we'll clean the rooms on a rota.'

'Good idea,' Mrs Kendrick agreed. The cook had warmed towards Lilah considerably and when the latter heard Moira mutter something about 'slave-drivers' one day, the cook had snarled at the maid to mind her manners.

Things were looking up.

The fact that she still missed Hamish was something Lilah tried to forget. She buried herself in work, finding all manner of tasks that needed doing – mending, accounts, ordering of supplies and things like making candles and sorting out the stillroom. She had been taught to make all the things necessary to a household such as soap, lavender water and herbal remedies. The gardener seemed happy to supply her with whatever she needed and she spent many happy hours making various concoctions, as well as different types of soap.

'Mmm, smells heavenly,' Mrs Kendrick said when given a small wash-ball from Lilah's first batch. 'Any guests coming here will like that, I should think. Lavender, is it?'

'Well, it's for all of us,' Lilah said and gave some to the other women as well. For Jameson and Armstrong she'd made a different type with a more manly smell that was scented with pine resin, which they seemed to like. Mr Findlay, although polite, had declined her offer saying he always bought his own. But since he appeared not to resent her presence, she didn't take this as an insult, merely his preference.

They were all seated in the kitchen having supper one evening when a commotion was heard from the yard. Jameson got up, shoving the last corner of a piece of bread into his mouth. 'I'll go see what's happening,' he said.

'No, sit, lad. I'll see to it,' Findlay ordered.

'Perhaps I'd better go as well in case rooms are needed.' Lilah followed him to the front of the house and out onto the steps that led into the courtyard where she'd first entered.

A horse and cart had drawn up next to them and a surly man was busy hefting a small trunk off the back, while a young boy jumped down from the other side. Findlay exchanged a puzzled glance with Lilah and shrugged, then they both descended into the courtyard and waited for the boy to come forward. 'Good afternoon,' Findlay said. 'Are you looking for someone?'

'Yes, Lord Blackwood. He lives here, doesn't he?'

Findlay frowned. 'It's his property, certainly, but he's not here now. May I ask who you are, young man?'

'I'm Tom. Thomas Whitley. Lord Blackwood is my guardian. Where is he?' This final question came out almost as a wail and Lilah gathered the poor boy was desperate to see his lordship. The sight of his distress made her want to protect him instantly. She decided it was time to intervene.

'I believe he's in London or perhaps at his estate in Wiltshire,' she told him. 'Your guardian, you say? I wasn't aware he had a ward.' Lilah was surprised at this turn of events. She hadn't figured Hamish for the kind of man who took on children and this boy couldn't be more than twelve or thirteen. 'How old are you?'

'I'm turned thirteen.' Tom was trying to look belligerent now but Lilah could see he was perilously close to tears and totally exhausted. The angry front was sheer bravado.

'And you've travelled here on your own?'

'Yes, from Edinburgh. I … I was sure his lordship would be here. He said to write to him here if I needed anything, but I had to see him instead so …'

'So you thought to come in person. I see. Well, why don't we get you inside? I'm sure you could do with a bite of supper and then we can write to his lordship to let him know you've arrived.' She turned to the butler. 'What do you think, Mr Findlay? He's due to come back here soon, isn't he?' Lilah didn't know that for sure, but wanted to calm the boy. She put a hand on his shoulder and gave it a squeeze. She had the urge to hug him instead, but restrained herself. In her experience, limited though it was, boys his age didn't appreciate such gestures no matter how tired they were.

'Yes, I believe so,' Findlay agreed.

'I can stay?' Tom's face brightened.

'Of course. I'm sure any ward of Lord Blackwood's is welcome here.'

Findlay nodded. 'I'll have Master Whitby's trunk taken up to the guest room nearest the master bedroom, shall I? Then we can continue our meal.'

'Ahem.' The surly man who'd driven the cart made his presence known. 'Beggin' yer pardon, Sir, Miss, but this here varmint has only paid me for half the journey. Said I'd be paid on arrival.'

Lilah looked to Tom for confirmation and he nodded while a blush spread over his thin cheeks. 'I didn't have enough for the whole fare,' he muttered.

'Very well. One moment, please, and we'll fetch the steward,' Lilah said. 'I'm sure he'll sort it out. Thank you for bringing Master Whitby safely to us.' She gave the man a nod and swept Tom away up the stairs and straight to the kitchen.

'Mrs Kendrick, here's someone who'll appreciate your lovely cooking. May we have an extra plate, please?'

Tom sank onto a chair, looking more cheerful. When he'd finished eating, Lilah led him up to the guest chamber. She closed the door behind her – the time had come for some answers.

'So why are you really here, Tom?' she asked in as gentle a voice as she could make it.

'What? Oh, er, I told you, I needed to see his lordship.' Tom's face was once again covered in a tell-tale blush and he wouldn't look Lilah in the eye.

'Shouldn't you be at school? Term time isn't finished yet, as far as I know.'

Tom muttered something.

'What was that? I can't help you if you don't tell me the truth, Tom.'

'I said, I was sent down. Well, expelled actually. For good.' The boy sank onto the bed and dug the toe of his shoe into the thick carpet, kicking at it. There was an audible catch in his voice, as though he was close to tears but trying valiantly not to cry.

'Oh dear, that's unfortunate. What did you do to deserve that?' Lilah didn't think Tom was the kind of boy who'd be bad on purpose. He seemed sweet and a bit shy rather than evil.

Tom sighed. 'Put manure in the headmaster's desk,' he muttered.

A splutter of laughter escaped Lilah before she tried to school her features into a more serious expression. 'R-really?' she stuttered, biting her lip. It seemed like the kind of prank most boys would relish but Tom had obviously had the misfortune of being caught.

'You don't seem angry,' Tom said, staring at her. 'The Headmaster was furious. Caned me something terrible, but of course I deserved that. Wasn't all my fault though. It was a dare.'

'I see. From whom?'

'Some of the older boys. They said unless I did it they'd make my life miserable for the next few years so I had no choice, do you see?' Tom blinked and rubbed absently at his back, which Lilah imagined must still be sore.

'Yes, I understand. Well, no matter, I'm sure his lordship will sort it out. I dare say he wasn't a saint himself when he was your age.' Lilah sincerely hoped that was true and that he wouldn't be too hard on the boy. She'd have to try to intervene, if so, as she'd already taken a liking to young Tom.

'He might punish me as well,' Tom said, his expression gloomy. 'Told me to behave at school to make my parents proud and I swore I would. But now ...'

'Tom, sometimes things happen that are out of our control. I'm sure Lord Blackwood will understand. I'll help you explain if you like.'

'Would you? Thank you, Miss, that would be most kind.'

'Not at all. And it's Mrs Robarts. Now why don't you have a little rest and then come and find me in the morning? We'll have to think of something for you to do while you're here. I doubt his lordship will want you sitting around idle.'

'Whatever you say, Miss, er, Mrs Robarts.'

'Good, that's settled then.'

Little by little, Tom's story became clearer. Lilah found out that he was the son of one of Lord Blackwood's closest friends, who'd had the misfortune to die of some tropical disease after he and his wife went travelling abroad. Tom's mother succumbed shortly afterwards.

'Always wanted to travel the world,' Tom said, 'and they'd promised to take me with them when I was older. But I had to have an education first, they were adamant about that.'

Lilah felt for him as he'd obviously been left behind many times and she could see he'd considered himself left out. 'A good thing you had Lord Blackwood as your guardian then, isn't it?'

'Yes, he was a great help when … In short, he took care of everything for me and I went to his Wiltshire house for a while to … to recover. But of course I had to go back to school eventually. One can't mope forever, you know.'

This last sentence was uttered with bravado, as if it was something the boy had repeated to himself to give courage. Lilah assumed it was what Hamish had told him and it seemed to have worked.

'Quite right too,' she agreed.

Tom proved to be extremely good with numbers, so Lilah made him help her with the household accounts, even though she could do them herself without any trouble. She also arranged for Mr Armstrong to give the boy some Latin lessons, and for the grooms to take him riding daily. She thought it best to keep him occupied so he didn't get into any more scrapes. In the meantime, she wrote to Hamish, both at his London address and the Wiltshire estate, to apprise him of Tom's arrival and asking what to do.

She hoped it wouldn't be long before she received a reply although secretly she was hoping Hamish would come to Scotland to deal with the matter himself.

'I, Delilah Eleonor Risden, take this man to be my lawful wedded husband …'

Deborah repeated the words after the blacksmith and tried not to let the laughter bubble up inside her. She was standing in the blacksmith's forge at Gretna Green with Jonathan Morwell, the younger son of the local squire, and she had him completely convinced that he was doing the right thing in pretending to be marrying her sister. It was an exceedingly cunning plan.

It had been so easy to persuade him, the silly fool. She'd returned to the country with her mother, then immediately ridden out on her own, finding Jonathan in his father's stables as was his wont. The young man was horse mad and talked of nothing but breeding, stud horses, pedigree and other such boring matters. And he wasn't the brightest of men either. In fact, he was exceedingly dim which was why he was perfect for her plan.

'Jonathan,' she'd hissed, pleased to have found him on his own with no grooms in attendance. 'It's me, Deborah.' They'd all known each other since childhood and didn't stand on ceremony, which was to her advantage now.

He looked up from the horse's hoof he'd been inspecting and threw her a startled glance. 'Deborah! What are you doing here? Everyone's saying that ... I mean, after what happened, I didn't think to see you out and about.'

'I didn't do anything wrong,' Deborah hissed, momentarily annoyed. 'I was the wronged party, remember?'

'Yes, well ...' Jonathan scratched his head as if he wasn't quite convinced about that, but Deborah continued swiftly.

'Never mind that now. The fact of the matter is I need your help.'

'Really?'

'Yes. Lilah has disappeared and I must make her come back. She was lying, as I'm sure you've realised, and if I can just get her to apologise publicly I can go back to London with my reputation intact and find a better husband.'

Jonathan blinked. 'I know no such thing. Apparently Delilah said that she had, er, allowed Lord Blackwood to take liberties. Why would she say that if it wasn't the truth?'

'Think, Jonathan! To thwart me, of course. You know we've always been at loggerheads and she simply couldn't bear to see me land such a great catch so she made it up. But she cut off her nose to spite her face, the silly girl, and now she's been forced to find employment. We have to save her, even though it's more than she deserves.'

'Right.' Jonathan looked confused. 'And …?'

'Well, you see, I know where she is. And I'm sure that if she came home a respectably married woman, my parents would forgive her. *I* would forgive her, as long as she retracted what she said about me publicly.'

'So what does this have to do with me?'

Deborah walked over to him and put a hand on his arm, looking up from under her lashes. 'Jonathan, I know it's a lot to ask, but in the past you have been kind enough to offer for her and I was wondering if … No, I shouldn't ask it of you. It's too much after what she did. I'm sorry, forget I mentioned it. I'm being selfish.'

She made her lower lip wobble and managed to squeeze out a tear as she turned away, shoulders slumped in seeming dejection.

'Deborah! You know I'd do anything for you and Delilah, anything at all. I can't bear to see you so unhappy. What would you have me do?'

'Will you marry Lilah?'

'What? How? I mean, she's not even here.'

'She doesn't need to be. I have a plan. The thing is, she's in Scotland, so we will have to fetch her back. On the way, you can marry her at Gretna Green and then she can come home a married woman.'

Jonathan was frowning, obviously trying to follow her reasoning. 'But she's always refused me. Why would she accept my suit now?' He sounded incredulous, as well he might, Deborah thought. No woman in her right mind would shackle herself to him unless she too was crazy about horses. He had nothing to offer, being a younger son, and effectively worked as his father's stud manager for free.

'We simply won't ask her. I will take the vows on her behalf. After all, who would know the difference except you? Then we'll show her the marriage lines and she'll have to go with you as she'll be legally yours. What do you say? Isn't that just perfect?'

He shook his head. 'I don't know, Deborah, she might not be best pleased.'

'But she won't have a choice. Think of her reputation – surely she'd rather be married to you than working as a lowly servant?'

'Well, perhaps.'

'Of course she would. And haven't you always wanted her? So what does it matter how it's done? She'll soon realise you've done her an enormous favour. Now she's tried the life of a servant, I'm sure she'll be very grateful to escape the drudgery. As long as you don't mind the scandal she's created?' Deborah stroked his arm slowly, batting her lashes again. 'Or am I asking too much of you?'

'No.' Jonathan smiled. 'To hell with scandal, begging your pardon! If I could have Delilah's hand in marriage, what do I care about such things? It's not as though I have a position in society to uphold anyway.'

'Oh, thank you! You're such a good man and as your wife, Lilah would once again be welcome in society.'

He beamed at her. 'I'll make sure of it, don't you worry. Now, let me just go and tell my father the good news and then we can—'

'No, Jonathan, you mustn't tell anyone. We'll have to go away secretly, like an elopement. Your father would never let you marry Lilah now, don't you see?'

'Oh, well, yes, I suppose …'

She stepped closer to him, taking both his hands. 'It won't take us long to go to Gretna though. I have some pin money saved which will take care of the expense and then when we come back, everyone will have to accept yours and Lilah's marriage as a *fait accompli*. Are you game?'

'Dash it all, why not?' He grinned at her. 'When do we go?'

'Meet me at the crossroads early tomorrow morning. I'll hire a carriage as I don't want to borrow Papa's. And I'll bring Dawson, my maid, so there's no impropriety.'

'Very well, I'll be there.'

And he had been. In fact, it had all gone very smoothly and she was Mrs Morwell, albeit temporarily. Because the certificate the smith made them sign said Delilah Risden, not Deborah, and now all she had to do was to somehow change positions with her sister.

Chapter Nine

'What are you doing, Moira?'

Lilah had just walked into the steward's office, closely followed by Tom. They'd wanted to ask Mr Armstrong if Tom's studies for the following day could be postponed so that Tom could go riding with Lilah as she had the afternoon off then, but he wasn't there. Instead they'd found Moira with her hands in one of the desk drawers. The maid jumped and gave a little shriek.

'N-nothin'. Just dustin'.' Moira's pale face was suffused with colour though and Lilah didn't believe her.

'Show me the contents of your apron pocket,' she ordered.

Moira shook her head. 'Why should I? There's nothin' in there.'

'If there isn't then you haven't anything to fear. So show me.' Lilah wasn't backing down. The woman may dislike her, but this was different. Mr Armstrong kept money in that drawer, she'd seen it. And Moira had no reason to dust inside it as she well knew.

Moira backed away and tried to dart round the desk. Lilah and Tom both moved to block the doorway. 'Show me what's in your pocket or I'm calling Mr Findlay,' Lilah said, quietly but firmly.

With a black glare, Moira tossed her head. 'Suit yerself.' She held out her apron so Lilah could see into the pocket. There was a handful of silver and gold coins, more money than Moira would earn in months.

'Tom, go and fetch Mr Findlay, please.' Lilah found that she was shaking, but tried not to show it. This was really unpleasant and not something she'd thought to have to deal with.

'Yes, Mrs Robarts, right away.'

The boy ran off and Lilah was left staring at Moira. She frowned at the woman. 'Why?' she asked. She wanted to understand. It wasn't as though Moira had been mistreated here. She worked a lot less than some servants, as Lilah well knew, and so far she'd been lenient with her.

'Ye wouldn't understand. We don't all have rich lovers,' Moira sneered.

'You're wrong about me, you know. I heard you talking about me behind my back and it's not true. Lord Blackwood has never laid so much as a finger on me.'

'A likely tale. I know what I saw,' Moira replied.

Lilah didn't think there was any point arguing about it. Moira had made up her mind. And now she'd have to leave in any case.

Tom returned, faster than Lilah had hoped, bringing Findlay who was scowling mightily. 'What's this I hear? Moira, what have you done now, you stupid girl?'

'Nothin'. Her high-and-mightiness is makin' up tales 'bout me on account of her not likin' me. Thinks I'm lazy.'

'I never said that,' Lilah protested.

'Ye didn't have to. I could see it in yer face.'

'Enough!' Findlay barked. 'Did you or did you not steal money from Mr Armstrong's drawer?'

95

'No.'

Lilah and Tom both gasped, then Tom spluttered, 'But we saw her, Mr Findlay, both of us! She had her hands in the drawer and now she's got the money in her apron.'

'Give me your apron, Moira.'

The woman untied it and handed it over slowly, then pointed at Lilah. 'She put the coins in there earlier, hopin' to blame me, and I was just puttin' them back.'

Lilah and Tom exchanged looks and shook their heads almost in unison.

Thankfully, Findlay took no notice of Moira and her lies. He took her roughly by the arm and marched her off towards the kitchen. 'I've had enough of you, girl. Always making trouble. Unless you want to be reported to the magistrate for theft and shipped off to the colonies or worse, I'd suggest you pack your things and leave. *Now.*'

Moira threw Lilah one last death-glare over her shoulder and Lilah shivered. She wasn't used to being hated that much, except by Deborah, but that was a different matter.

Findlay came back soon after and asked to speak to Lilah in private. Tom made himself scarce.

'I've asked Jameson to make sure that woman leaves immediately,' he said, as soon as they were alone. 'I hope you didn't mind me taking matters into my own hands? I realise she was under your jurisdiction and I should have asked your opinion.'

'No, don't worry, I don't mind at all. In fact, I want to thank you for not believing her. I know she resented my presence here, but I had hoped she'd come to accept me eventually.'

Findlay shook his head. 'No chance of that, I'm afraid. She's always been a lazy girl and that's why she got on all right with old Mrs McDuff who never noticed. Neither did Cook, as she had too much to do and couldn't chase up the maids all the time. And this isn't the first time things have gone missing.'

'Oh?'

'Cook noticed a few items gone from the larder and it was always on the day before Moira had a day off. We put two and two together, but as she comes from a poor home, we decided to let it go. This, however, was unacceptable. I should have taken her to the magistrate, but the punishments are so harsh. Not really what you'd wish on your worst enemy ...'

'I agree and I'm glad you didn't. We won't mention this to anyone and hopefully Moira will have learned her lesson. She'll have to find another place to work now and there's no harm done as the money never left the premises.'

'Quite so.' He gave her a small smile. 'Thank you, I'm glad we are in agreement.'

Lilah went to find Tom and sincerely hoped that was the end of the matter.

'Dear Lord, but this is a godforsaken part of the country, isn't it?' Deborah was looking around at the stark scenery they were travelling through and thought to herself that she'd never have agreed to so much as visit this place if she'd become Lady Blackwood. She would have chosen to remain at his lordship's main estates down south. There wasn't a soul for miles here so who on earth would you socialise with?

'It's beautiful in a wild sort of way,' Jonathan murmured, but he knew better than to argue outright with Deborah.

He'd been rather quiet the last day or so, as they continued north towards Lord Blackwood's estate in the Highlands. Deborah hoped he wasn't getting cold feet, but even if he was, it was too late. She hadn't quite decided how to implement the last part of her plan yet, but she knew she'd think of something. First though, she wanted to *reconnoitre*, although she would stay out of sight as much as possible. To that end, she was wearing a cape with a hood which she'd pulled up to shield most of her face.

Just as they reached a crossroads where they'd been told to take a left for the Blackwood lands, a red-headed woman came marching along the road. Judging by the way she was dressed, she was a servant and she was quite clearly in a temper as she kicked at the odd stone from time to time while muttering to herself. Deborah banged on the carriage roof to make the coachman stop and he reined in next to the woman.

Deborah decided it probably didn't matter if she showed her face to a lowly maid-servant and pulled down the window.

'Excuse me, but could you tell me whether we're on the right road for Lord Blackwood's house?'

The woman looked up and froze, her eyes growing huge in her pale face. She took a step backwards. 'Ye!' she spat. 'Am I never to be free of ye? Leave me alone or so help me ...'

Deborah started to laugh. She knew exactly what was going on here as it wasn't the first time it had happened. 'I think you're mistaking me for my sister,' she said. 'I'm Deborah, not Delilah. Who are you?'

'What? There's two of ye?'

'Yes, we're twins. Not that unusual, is it? Now answer my question, please.'

'Oh, I'm Moira. Moira Grant and if ye'll pardon me, I'd rather not speak to anyone in yer family right now, seein' as yer sister just lost me my position.' The woman picked up her bundle of belongings, which she'd rested on the ground as they spoke, and prepared to leave.

'Did she now? That's interesting.' Deborah had a great idea. 'Hold on a moment. As you don't seem to like my sister very much, perhaps you'd like to take your revenge on her?'

'Revenge? How?' Moira looked up again.

'If you'll come with us to the nearest inn, I'll tell you. I have a plan, you see.'

'Deborah, what are you up to now?' Jonathan entered the conversation for the first time, having remained quiet so far. 'I thought you said we'd just go and tell Delilah of her good fortune and—'

'I've changed my mind,' Deborah interrupted him. 'I don't think that's such a good idea. Far better if we get her away from here first and on her way home with you, then you can tell her.' She smiled at Moira, who seemed to be listening avidly. 'And this kind woman is just the person to help us, I believe.'

'Very well, but it'll cost ye,' Moira said, staring from one to the other, her scowl having let up a little.

'I'm sure we can come to some agreement,' Deborah

assured her. 'Jonathan, open the door please. Come in, Moira. It'll be faster that way. You can sit next to Dawson.'

Jonathan did as he was asked, as always.

Lilah sat in the window embrasure of her room with a pile of sheets that needed mending. Her other tasks this morning were done and she quite enjoyed the peace and solitude of sitting here on a sunny day with the gorgeous view of the loch spread before her whenever she looked up. She'd never minded sewing and prided herself on her small, neat stitches. It didn't feel like a chore to her at all.

She'd come to realise that being a housekeeper wasn't a bad life, especially if, like her, you didn't mind hard work. As she had acted impulsively at the wedding and thrown caution to the wind, things could have gone much worse afterwards. In fact, she didn't even want to think about where she might have ended up – a young and inexperienced girl with no references and no one to help her. She could have stayed and faced her parents' – and her sister's – wrath, but they would have punished her, and her life as she'd known it would have been over. Even if they'd allowed her to stay, it would no longer have been as their daughter, but a social pariah. At least now she was independent and earning her keep and no one here knew about her past.

A knock on the door brought Shona with a tray set with the tea caddy, hot water, a cup and saucer and a plate of biscuits. She looked anxious and her hands were shaking a little, but Lilah knew the young girl was still finding her feet in the household and sometimes found it difficult to cope with all that was asked of her. 'Cook's lying down on account of a megrim so lunch will be a bit late, so I … thought I'd bring ye this, Mrs Robarts.'

'Thank you, that's very kind. What's happening about the meal then? Shall I come and help you?' Lilah took the tray from the maid and set it on a table near the window.

'No, I'll manage, thank ye. There's cold pie, bread and cheese, so I'll just boil some potatoes to make a mash.'

'Excellent. Call me if you need me.'

Shona left quickly, as if she couldn't get away fast enough, muttering something that sounded like 'I'm sorry'. Lilah wondered why. The girl wasn't normally afraid of her but today she wouldn't even look her in the eye. Strange. She measured out the tea from the caddy, to which only she and Cook had the key, then poured herself a cup, adding milk. She leaned back against the stone wall of the window seat and took a big sip.

The tea didn't taste as good as she'd thought it would, being slightly bitter. Lilah looked inside the tea caddy, wondering if this consignment had been bad in some way, but it looked and smelled the same as always. 'How odd,' she muttered and took another sip. Still the same.

To offset the weird taste, she ate two biscuits, which helped her drink the rest of her cup, but she decided not to have a second one. There was definitely something not right about this.

'I'll have to speak to Mrs Kendrick, see if she's noticed anything,' she murmured to herself.

Picking up her mending, she tried to concentrate on her sewing once more, but for some reason she was having trouble focusing now. Her stitches weren't so neat any longer and she kept yawning and blinking as her eyelids suddenly felt very heavy. Why was she so tired? She hadn't done much physical work today.

Perhaps she'd just lean her head against the window for a moment until the tiredness passed ...

Chapter Ten

Hamish rode down the road towards Coille Dubh with an urgency he couldn't explain even to himself. He'd received Lilah's letter about Tom and wondered what the little varmint had done to get himself expelled from school. Lilah hadn't said, only that she'd let Tom explain it in his own words. Hamish hoped it wasn't something really bad as he liked the boy and felt sorry for him. Tom had gone through a lot in the last year so he didn't want to be too harsh with him.

He had to admit he was glad to have an excuse to return. Ever since he'd left for the south, he'd had a feeling he shouldn't have done and the urge to go back was strong. But he knew he had to leave Lilah in Scotland at least for a while to see how she fared. If being his housekeeper was truly all she'd wanted from him, she was a remarkable woman and one he could be proud to admire. But if not … then perhaps her letter had just been a ruse to make him come back so she could make other demands?

He wished he knew which it was.

A groom came running to take the reins of his horse and led the stallion away as soon as Hamish entered the courtyard. He took the stairs up to the hall two at a time and was met by the ever efficient Findlay. 'Good afternoon, my lord. I trust you had a smooth journey?' the butler said, closing the door behind Hamish.

'Yes, thank you. My valet will be arriving tomorrow. I rode ahead of him.'

'Ah, so he turned up eventually?'

'Yes, I met him when I travelled to London last time. He'd almost reached here, but I made him turn back.' Hamish smiled and added in a theatrical whisper, 'He's not best pleased with me for making him come all the way back again so soon, but don't tell him I told you.'

Findlay permitted himself a small smile in return.

'So what has been going on here then? I gather my ward turned up rather unexpectedly. How is he?'

'The lad is very well, my lord. He's currently with Mr Armstrong, doing some Latin translation, I believe.'

'Excellent. And Mrs Robarts, has she settled in?'

Findlay frowned and looked away. 'Well, she had, my lord, but this afternoon things have not been to her liking, I gather.'

'What do you mean?' Lilah's letter had given him to understand that all was progressing well, but hearing the butler's words made Hamish instantly suspicious and, if he was honest with himself, disappointed.

'She, uhm, found fault with the food at lunchtime and the fact that it was late on account of Mrs Kendrick having a megrim. They had an argument, then Mrs Robarts told Shona off for being insolent when she tried to defend Cook. Later she told young Tom not to bother her as she was "busy", though as far as I can tell she's merely been spending time in her room resting. Oh, and her room is apparently "smaller than a monk's cell", something she's never mentioned before.' Findlay shook his head. 'I'm afraid I can't understand it, but then women seem to be a law unto themselves.'

'Hmm, indeed. I shall have to have a word with her.

Could you please inform her of my arrival? And bring some refreshment. I'll see her in here.'

Shona arrived first with a tray of wine and macaroons and just after she'd left, Delilah swept into the room. Hamish noticed she was wearing the black silk dress he'd bought her, even though she'd told him she would keep it for Sunday best. Today was a Wednesday.

'Hamish, you're back at last! I thought you'd never come.'

To his amazement, she rushed forward and threw her arms around his neck, burying her head in his shoulder. He blinked.

'Delilah! The servants ...'

She looked up, her beautiful silver eyes shining. 'Oh, never mind them, they're all in the kitchen I'm sure. I've been so lonely without you.' She lifted her mouth for a kiss and Hamish didn't have the willpower to resist just then. Truth to tell, he'd missed her terribly and he had dreamed of holding her in his arms again. She was a very pleasing armful, no doubt about that. But more than that, he'd come to realise he enjoyed her company and he had been lonely too.

Something about their kiss didn't ring true though and while he tried to lose himself in it, at the same time something niggled at the back of his mind. After a while it hit him – this kiss was much too knowing.

When he'd kissed Delilah that time at the inn, she'd been clueless, not moving her mouth against his or welcoming his touch in any way. She had acted like someone who had never been kissed in her life. Today, however, she was more or less inviting him to kiss her more deeply, seducing him with her lips, while her luscious body was moulded to his. He broke off the kiss and stared into her eyes. The innocence and lack of guile he'd come to associate with Delilah were not there. Instead he saw a glint of something – passion, triumph, cunning? He wasn't sure. He was certain of one thing though – this wasn't the Delilah he'd come to admire. What had happened to her while he'd been gone?

Disappointment flooded him at the thought that he'd been right not to trust her. It had all been an act and now she'd had enough.

'Delilah,' he murmured, wary now, 'this is rather … unexpected. I hadn't thought to receive quite such a warm welcome.'

'Oh, Hamish, I didn't think you'd leave me here for so long.'

He frowned. 'I did say I wouldn't be back until August.'

'Did you? It must have slipped my mind.' She gave a high-pitched giggle that sounded nothing like the delightful sound she'd made when he was helping to pin up her hem. She tried to pull his head back down for another kiss but Hamish hesitated. This felt all wrong.

Another possibility struck him and he decided to put it to the test.

'Delilah,' he said again and bent his head to nuzzle her neck, just below the jaw line on her left hand side. 'We really shouldn't, not here …'

'Oh, Hamish, please …'

He used his fingers to tilt her head up a little more, as if he wanted to find a better spot to kiss her neck. At the same time he checked the smooth skin and what he sought definitely wasn't there. The faint scar Delilah had shown him once was gone.

This was not Delilah. Relief surged through him at the same time as a wave of anger. Deborah. How dare she?

Hamish was in a quandary. On the one hand, he wanted to shove this woman as far away from himself as possible. Deborah had tricked him once, he wouldn't let her do it again. She disgusted him. But on the other, if she was here pretending to be her sister, where was Delilah? And what was Deborah hoping to achieve by switching places with her twin? He very much doubted she was after employment as a humble housekeeper.

His immediate instinct was to try and shake the truth out of her, but he'd never been violent towards a woman in his life and he wasn't about to start now. No, this called for stealth. He should probably wait for the devious lady to reveal her intentions without letting on that he knew who she was. At least not yet. He felt sure that she was going to use some underhand method to force him to comply with her wishes. Perhaps she was holding Delilah hostage somewhere, hoping he would agree to marriage on condition no harm came to his housekeeper? Although why she thought he would care, he had no idea.

He fought hard to quell the anger that continued to rise inside him. If she so much as hurt one hair on Delilah's head he'd ... Well, he didn't know what he'd do, but it wouldn't be pleasant.

'Let us have some wine,' he said, stalling for time.

She must have an accomplice of some sort. Hamish very much doubted Deborah could spirit away her sister single-handedly. He could only hope that whoever she'd hired to do her dirty work kept Delilah safe until such time as Deborah gave him or her a signal.

Hamish clenched his jaw. He'd give the woman one night to reveal her intent, but if she hadn't told him by morning what she'd done with her twin, he would make her, one way or another.

Lilah woke up with a pounding head and a foul taste in her mouth. She kept her eyes shut in the hope that the pounding would lessen, but after a while she came to realise that it wasn't just inside her head. She was in a moving carriage and the rhythmic noise was the sound of horses' hooves hitting the ground and wheels banging on stones.

Her eyes flew open and promptly shut again as daylight hit her and sent a shaft of pain through her brain. She groaned.

'Ah, you're awake at last! I was beginning to think the laudanum would never wear off.'

Lilah cracked open one eyelid again and squinted at the person sitting opposite her. 'Jonathan?'

She seemed to by lying on one seat while he was on the other, but he moved across now and helped her into a sitting position. He groped inside a basket by his feet and held out a flask for her. 'Here, have some water. I'm told it will help wake you up.'

Lilah just stared at him. '*Jonathan?* What on earth are you doing here? Where am I? What …?'

'Whoa, one question at a time.' He held up a hand. 'Here, drink first.'

She shook her head but regretted it as the imaginary

sledgehammer began to beat her brain again. 'I'm not drinking anything unless I know what's in it. What did you do to me? Laudanum, did you say? I thought that was Deborah's favourite way of …' She tailed off and her eyes widened as she saw him wince. 'No! This was her idea, wasn't it? She drugged me? Why the little … I am going to kill her for this.'

'Now, now, calm down, Delilah. It was for your own good. We've saved you, you see.' Jonathan held up his hands, as if to soothe her the way he did his precious horses.

'Saved me? How?' Lilah couldn't believe this was happening. How had her sister found her? And more importantly, how had she managed to drug her in Lord Blackwood's house?

Then she remembered Shona and her refusal to look Lilah in the eye. Had Deborah bribed the girl? Threatened her? Either way, it was clear she'd made her administer the drug. Lilah wanted to throttle her sister with her bare hands. How dare she?

And was she never to be free of Deborah?

Jonathan touched her arm tentatively. 'It's not as bad as you might think. You're safe with me and I'm going to save your reputation. In fact, I've already done so. Look here.'

He brought out a piece of paper from an inside pocket and held it out for Lilah. She took it and tried to focus on the writing. At first, she couldn't make it out, but after blinking a few times she was able to read it.

'A marriage solemnised at Gretna Green on … Jonathan Charles Morwell, Esquire, son of Sir Charles Morwell, Baronet and Delilah Eleonor Risden. *Delilah*

Eleonor!' She stared up at Jonathan who was smiling and nodding as if the piece of paper held the key to the greatest of happiness. And perhaps it did for him, but definitely not for her. Lilah scowled at him, ignoring the pain that shot through her brow as she did so. 'What is the meaning of this, Jonathan? I have *not* married you and you know it. I think I would have remembered so momentous an occasion, don't you?'

'Oh, but that's the beauty of the plan,' Jonathan explained, slowly as if he was talking to a five-year old who was unable to grasp simple facts. 'You didn't have to be present because Deborah did it for you! You look so alike, it was easy. Now all we have to do is go home and show everyone this and they'll be pleased for us. As my wife, you can take your rightful place in society again and the silly scandal will be forgotten.' His expression clouded over slightly. 'Well, after you tell everyone you didn't mean what you said, of course. We can't have people thinking I married Lord Blackwood's leftovers.'

Lilah glared at him. 'Wonderful. And I take it Deborah came up with this? I can't believe you'd be quite so devious. I thought we were friends.' She couldn't quite keep the accusing note out of her voice. She *had* thought they were friends and that he'd understood why she couldn't marry him. She didn't love him.

'We are.' He looked hurt. 'And that's why I'm doing this. To help you. Deborah explained it all and it made so much sense. You need me so really you don't have a choice. A little gratitude wouldn't go amiss. Surely you wouldn't rather work as a scullery maid than be my wife?'

Lilah thought he resembled nothing so much as a

big, dozy puppy, and she didn't want to hurt him, but there seemed to be no choice. 'Yes, I would,' she replied bluntly.

'What?' His mouth fell open.

'I wasn't working as a scullery maid, you fool,' she hissed. 'I have a respectable job as housekeeper and I'm very sorry but I much prefer that to falling in with my sister's grand plans. Now please, take me back.'

'But Delilah, you can't mean that. Think about your reputation, the life you could have with me.'

'I *am* thinking of it,' Lilah muttered, then raised her voice. 'Turn this carriage around this instant, or I'm getting out to walk.'

Jonathan's mouth set in a stubborn line and he shook his head. 'I'm afraid I can't do that. Deborah said you might become obstinate and I wasn't to pay you any heed. It's for your own good and for your family's honour. I'm not letting you go anywhere except home with me.'

Lilah narrowed her eyes at him but realised he'd been primed by her sister and there would be no way of reasoning with him. Very well, she'd have to think of another way because nothing on earth would make her live as Jonathan's wife. She really would rather be a scullery maid, in truth.

'Have it your way,' she said, shuffling over to one side of the seat as far away from him as possible. 'But I'll never willingly tell anyone I agreed to this or that I'm your wife. In fact, I'm not speaking to you again.'

Jonathan glared back, stubbornness etched across his features. 'Yes, you will, but Deborah said I was to give you some time to get used to the idea so that's what

I'll do. I'm going to have a nap now and I sincerely hope you're in a better frame of mind when I wake up.'

He shuffled back to the other seat, crossed his arms over his chest and closed his eyes, his mouth in a thin angry line. Lilah almost smiled as he looked like a little child that's been denied a treat.

But as soon as his eyes were closed, she took the document which she still held in her hands and folded it as small as she could. Then she stuffed it inside her bodice. The moment they reached an inn, she intended to get rid of it.

Deborah seemed determined to stay by Hamish's side and he finally had to resort to a none-too-subtle hint. 'Don't you have some duties to perform as my housekeeper, Delilah? I daresay Cook needs to be supervised so that she doesn't burn my supper. And you'll want to check whether my room has been prepared the way I like it, won't you?'

Deborah frowned, obviously not best pleased to have to act as his servant, but she finally took herself off to oversee these matters. 'Yes, of course. But we can have supper together, can't we, just the two of us?' she purred just before leaving.

He dredged up a fake smile. 'I shall look forward to it, my love.'

He didn't know why she seemed to think that his and Delilah's relationship had progressed to the stage of being lovers, but he'd decided to play along with it for now. He was interested to see where she was hoping to take this, although he was fairly certain he knew already. For Deborah, the aim had always been to become his Countess and he guessed that if she couldn't do so as herself, she'd try to do it in the guise of her twin.

As soon as she'd gone, he asked for Tom to be called to his study. After greeting the boy with a hug – not the conventional greeting for a ward, but with Tom alone in the world Hamish felt the boy needed to know that there was someone who cared about him – he went straight to the point.

'Now then, young Tom, what is this I hear – you've been expelled?'

'Yes, my lord.' Tom stood before him and stared at the carpet, scuffing it slightly with one booted toe. 'I'm very sorry to have let you down.' He stammered out a confession of what he'd done.

'You haven't let me down, but yourself,' Hamish said gently. 'And I thought we agreed you'd call me Uncle Hamish? None of that "my lord" business, if you please.' Tom nodded but still didn't raise his head. 'Well, putting manure in the headmaster's desk doesn't sound like the sort of thing you'd normally get up to. Would you care to explain?'

Tom told Hamish about the dare and the older boys. 'But I know I shouldn't have done it even so.'

Hamish smiled. 'It doesn't seem to me as though you had a choice.' When Tom looked up at him at last, blinking in surprise, he added, 'I went to that kind of school myself, Tom. I know what it's like and there are always older boys picking on the younger ones. Either you stand up to them and get in trouble for fighting, or you do as they say and hope to get away with it. Unfortunately, this time you were caught and punished.

We'll say no more about it and we will find you another school for next term. All right?'

'Th-thank you, Uncle Hamish!' Tom's face broke into a huge smile and he rushed forward to throw his arms around Hamish's middle. 'Thank you.'

'Not at all. Now come and sit down and tell me what's been happening here. I understand from Findlay that you've had a slight, er, disagreement with my new housekeeper.'

They sat down and Tom frowned and shook his head. 'Yes, it's deuced odd, begging your pardon, but … We were getting on famously and Mrs Robarts was so kind to me when I arrived here. Arranged for me to have lessons with Mr Armstrong, asked the grooms to take me riding and generally cheered me up. But this afternoon she was like a different woman, cold and harsh. Didn't want me around. I … I don't know what I've done wrong, Uncle Hamish, and that's the truth.'

Hamish nodded. 'Actually, you haven't done anything and you're more right than you think. I'm going to tell you a secret, but only if you swear not to let on to anyone?'

'Of course, I swear.'

Hamish leaned forward and in a whisper told Tom of his suspicions.

'No! But that's terrible! And what's happened to—'

'Shhh, not a word, remember?'

'Oh, right, yes, sorry.' Tom lowered his voice. 'But what will you do? We have to help Mrs Robarts!'

'We will, but first I have to find out where she's been taken. I doubt her sister acted alone in this. Someone else must have spirited Delilah away somewhere.'

'You don't think she's …' Tom swallowed hard, his eyes huge with sudden fear.

'No, I doubt she'd go that far. Not yet anyway. We must keep our eyes and ears open until I can make her tell me the truth. Can you try and find out more from the servants? Maybe the grooms or gardener saw something earlier? That seems to have been when she supposedly "changed" so we can assume that's when they swapped places.'

'I'll go and talk to them immediately, sound them out.' Tom stood up, eager to go.

'Thank you, but be discreet. I'm waiting to see what the sister does next, but if necessary, I'll try to force her to reveal where Delilah has been taken. Off you go then. Come and report to me later, please.'

'I will.'

Chapter Eleven

Lilah dozed for a while as her head was still hurting and the carriage wasn't the best she'd ever been in. The springs were old and more or less worn out so every rut in the road jolted her painfully. She didn't think she had anything to fear from Jonathan at the moment. He'd never been violent and she was sure she could keep him at arm's length for a while by appealing to his kind nature.

They came to a halt at last and Lilah opened her eyes. It was late afternoon but still light and she could see that they had stopped by a small inn. It looked unprepossessing and none too clean. 'Are you short of funds?' Lilah asked Jonathan bluntly. No point beating about the bush. He'd never been rich and never would be.

'No. Well, yes. Look, I'm just trying to be frugal. No telling how long it will take us to get back home. Now, let's go inside. I'm sure the landlord will have a private parlour for us and some victuals.'

This proved to be true, although the room they were shown into had definitely seen better days. Lilah itched to grab a duster and broom to give it a good clean, but instead perched on a wooden chair with a wonky leg while the landlord's wife brought them some food.

'Pie, my favourite!' Jonathan thanked the woman in a falsely cheerful voice even though they could both see that the pie didn't look very appetising and the vegetables that had been served with it were limp and overcooked. He grabbed a bottle of wine the landlord had placed on the table and poured out two glasses. 'Here, let's have a toast to our happy future.'

Lilah lifted her eyebrows at him. 'You can't be serious?'

Jonathan sighed and sat down, taking a healthy swig from his wine. 'Please don't be difficult, Delilah. You must face the truth which is that you don't have a choice. You're my wife now and I promise I won't let anyone malign you. The scandal will soon die down and everything will go back to normal.'

She shook her head. 'Jonathan, you're the one who needs to realise something here – I'm *never* going to be your wife. I appreciate your gentlemanly sentiments and it's extremely kind of you to want to "rescue" me, but as I said earlier, I didn't need to be rescued. I was doing very well on my own and I'm perfectly happy working as a housekeeper.'

'You can't mean it. Why would you be?'

'It's simple – as Lord Blackwood's housekeeper I am being paid for my services whereas if I was your wife I'd be working all day every day for nothing. My dowry – provided my parents would still be willing to pay one out – would belong to you and we both know what you'd do with it: buy more horses. We'd be dependent upon your father for things like food, somewhere to live, even our clothes. You always have been and you always will be.'

'It's not as bad as all that …' Jonathan was frowning, but Lilah was sure he knew she was right. Deborah must have worked on him for days, however, as he rallied again. 'And anyway, it makes no difference –

you *are* my wife now and we can't change that so you'll have to make the best of it.'

'Actually, I'm not. Watch this,' Lilah said. She'd deliberately sat down closest to the meagre fire, which the landlady had stoked up before leaving the room. Lilah fished the marriage certificate out of her bodice and pushed it into the flames. 'There, that's your proof gone. We are no longer husband and wife.'

'Delilah, no!' He rushed over and tried to use the fire tongs to retrieve the document, but it was too late. It disappeared with a whoosh of flames and crumpled into a black ball. Jonathan turned on her. 'What did you do that for? Now we'll have to go all the way back to Gretna Green.'

Lilah sighed and stood up, pushing him away. 'For heaven's sake, Jonathan, can you just get it into your thick head that I don't want to be married to you. Go home! Forget I exist. And stop listening to Deborah. Don't you see? She's been using you for her own ends to punish me. Do you seriously think she cares what has become of me? Of course not!'

'She might do.' Jonathan had the air of a sulky five-year old.

'Don't be a fool. You know as well as I do that Deborah only thinks about what *she* wants. She's never cared about anyone else in her life. Why would she start now? No, this was revenge, pure and simple. Now are you going to take me back to the castle or do I have to walk?'

Hamish glanced at his dinner companion and lifted his glass of wine to his mouth, but he had no intention of drinking it. The memory of her lacing his tea with laudanum that last time was much too fresh in his mind. He needed to keep his wits about him this evening so he just pretended to take a sip now and then.

Tom had reported back to him that Moira had been seen by the gardener, walking with Mrs Robarts even though the maid had apparently been dismissed the previous day by Findlay. There had been something furtive about the two women, but neither had spoken to the gardener. Instead they had disappeared into the kitchens.

'Maybe Moira was helping Mrs Robarts' sister?' Tom had speculated. 'That was probably round the time when Mrs Kendrick was feeling poorly.'

'But there must have been other people around. Findlay? Shona? Or Jameson?'

'Maybe, but they could have been working elsewhere in the house. One of the grooms saw a strange carriage draw up by the back door, but he said it didn't stay long. He assumed it was a delivery of some sort, and although he offered to help hold the horses, the coachman apparently told him to clear off, so he did.'

'Hmm, so Delilah was definitely taken away from here. Thank you, at least we know that much then.'

Hamish had wondered whether she might have been locked into the cellar or somewhere like that but it had seemed unlikely Deborah would keep her sister on the premises.

Deborah was making eyes at him across the table. To her obvious annoyance, he'd insisted they should sit at opposite ends of the long expanse. 'It's highly irregular, you having dinner with me, you know,' he'd told her. 'We don't want the servants to gossip.'

'So, how are you settling in?' he asked now. 'I hope you've been getting along well with the other servants?'

Deborah pouted prettily. 'Well, we're not exactly meant to be friends, are we?' She tinkled out a laugh. 'They just have to do as I say.' She twirled the stem of her own wine glass. 'Although, to tell the truth, I'm a little weary of this charade. It's not what I'm used to, as you know.'

'It was your idea,' Hamish said.

'Was it? I mean, yes, of course, but I'm not sure I actually believed that you would … That is to say, it's very kind of you to bring me up to the wilds of Scotland, but it does get a little bit tedious here, doesn't it? And I didn't think it was to be a permanent arrangement.'

'Tedious? Do you think so? Actually, I beg to disagree. This is my favourite place on earth.'

'What?' Deborah's eyebrows rose, then she broke into laughter. 'Oh, I see, you're roasting me. That's too bad of you, but I forgive you.'

Hamish stared at her. How could she be that insensitive? So completely focused on herself? She really had no idea about his likes and dislikes and obviously cared even less. For now, he needed to play along with her though if he was to find out more.

'So what do you propose we do about it then? Would you rather be my housekeeper in Wiltshire? I suppose I could fire the one I have there, although she's frightfully efficient so it would be a shame.'

Deborah raised her wine glass and fluttered her eyelashes at him over the rim of it. 'Well, I was thinking more along the lines of a permanent solution. I can, of course, run your various households for you, but it would be much easier if I were to do it as your wife. And there would be other benefits too, of course …' She smiled, using the dimples either side of her mouth to full effect.

Hamish raised his eyebrows at her. 'But I doubt you have a dowry now and as an earl I shouldn't really be marrying someone tainted by scandal. Think of my reputation in the House of Lords.'

Deborah frowned. 'But I did it for you, Hamish. The scandal was for your benefit. You owe me more than a position as a mere housekeeper, don't you think?'

Hamish almost smiled. She was laying her cards on the table at last. 'I don't know …' He pretended to hesitate. 'It's very tempting. *You're* very tempting, but …'

She smiled at the flattery, perhaps feeling she was getting somewhere at last. Hamish didn't know for how long he should keep up the charade, but just then there was a knock on the door and Findlay came in looking unusually agitated.

'My lord, I beg your pardon, I am loath to disturb, but there's something of a crisis. If you could possibly come and advise us, just for a moment?'

'What is it, Findlay?' Hamish stood up.

'It's Armstrong, my lord. We think he may be having an apoplexy.'

'Really? Dear Lord …' Hamish turned to Deborah. 'Will you excuse me just for a short while, my dear? I'll be back as soon as I can.'

She nodded graciously. 'Of course. So tedious, always having to be the one in charge, isn't it? But a burden shared and all that …'

Hamish rushed out of the room before he shouted

at her that she was the last person on earth he'd share anything with. Bemused, he followed Findlay down to the kitchen, a room he didn't often visit. In the doorway, he stopped dead and just stared.

'Delilah! Oh, thank the Lord, you're safe!'

Lilah was standing in the middle of the kitchen with Jonathan behind her, still muttering about stubborn women in general and Risden females in particular. She saw a huge smile break out on Hamish's face as he caught sight of her and something inside her melted. She'd been so afraid he wouldn't know the difference between her and her twin, but he clearly recognised her.

'Ha—, er, my lord.' She curtseyed politely, the way a housekeeper should to her master, but then she couldn't help but smile in return. 'So you can tell then?'

He nodded, but as if to make quite sure he walked over to her and tilted her chin up. 'Yes, but I am heartily glad to see *that*.' One finger trailed the scar under her chin, giving her goosepimples all the way down her arm. 'Oh, dash it all,' he added, and swept her into his arms, giving her a bear hug that almost squashed her insides completely.

'I say!' Jonathan coughed pointedly. 'Damned irregular, no?'

Hamish seemed to realise that Jonathan was right and released Lilah slowly. She felt bereft and wished that she could have stayed in his arms forever, but it had obviously just been a momentary aberration. He'd been so pleased to find her safe, although why it should matter so much, she had no idea.

'What was he talking about?' Jonathan murmured.

Hamish fixed him with a glare. 'Delilah has a small scar, her sister doesn't. That's how you can tell them apart. And you are?'

Jonathan flushed bright red. 'Oh, er, Jonathan Morwell, at your service, my lord.' He executed a clumsy bow.

'Jon's a neighbour of ours from home,' Lilah explained. 'Deborah had him believing a whole faradiddle of nonsense, but we've sorted it out now, I believe. Is she still here?' She felt a stirring of unease at the thought of her sister at Coille Dubh. Had Deborah managed to sink her claws into Hamish again or did the fact that he recognised Lilah mean the ruse had failed?

'Yes, she's here. We were just having dinner.'

'D-dinner?' Lilah didn't like the sound of that. It sounded much too intimate and he'd refused to let her eat with him, so why grant Deborah the privilege?

'I'll explain, but perhaps we should go to my study? Quickly though, I need to get back to your sister.'

'Oh, right, of course.' Lilah was confused but she could see that it would be much better to discuss the matter in private, not in front of an audience consisting of Findlay, Jameson, Mrs Kendrick and a very frightened-looking Shona. As well she might be, Lilah thought darkly. She'd deal with the silly girl later.

Lilah and Jonathan followed Hamish and he closed the door behind them. She quickly filled him in on what had happened to her and when he seemed on the verge of doing violence to Jonathan for his part in her kidnapping, she put up a hand to restrain him. 'Please, my lord, there's no need. Jon merely did as Deborah asked him to, thinking he was helping me restore my honour and place in society. He understands now that

123

I'd rather stay here and I'm content with my life the way it is. Isn't that right, Jon?'

Jonathan sighed and shrugged his shoulders. 'Well, it seems deuced odd to me, but then all females are a mystery.'

Lilah turned to Hamish. 'So what happens now? Do we confront Deborah or what do you suggest?' He still hadn't explained why he'd been having dinner with her sister and Lilah didn't like the thought of them eating together so intimately.

Hamish was deep in thought and didn't answer immediately, but when he did, a small smile played about his mouth. 'Do you know, I think it's time Miss Deborah had a dose of her own medicine. I believe I have a plan.'

'Oh, good.' Lilah was all for punishing Deborah in some way, however small. She doubted it would change her sister's character much, but anything was better than just letting her ride away with Jonathan.

Hamish fixed Jon with a hard stare. 'Mr Morwell, in exchange for my not reporting you to the authorities on charges of abduction, might I count on your help with my plan?'

Jonathan flushed scarlet again. 'I say, my lord, I didn't intend any harm and—'

'Nevertheless, you did help to abduct my housekeeper and I believe the punishment for such activities is not pleasant.' Hamish's expression was grim, purposeful.

'P-perhaps, but ... oh, dash it all, I'll do whatever you wish me to. Only don't tell anyone about my part in this, I beg you. My father would flay me alive and then he'd never give me any of his blunt for the horses.'

'Very well. Then I must ask you – in exchange for a large sum of money, would you be prepared to marry Deborah, or at least ask her?'

'What?' Jonathan blinked. 'Why? I mean, she'd never agree, for one thing and begging your pardon, but she wouldn't exactly make a comfortable wife.'

Hamish's smile was not pleasant. 'Oh, believe me, I'm well aware of that. But it's up to you, of course. I can make it worth your while.'

'A large sum? How large?' Jonathan was clearly wavering and blanched when Hamish named an amount which would comfortably buy an entire stud farm, complete with several prize horses.

'That's if she agrees. If not, I'll still pay you a smaller amount for helping us to clear this mess up. What do you say?'

'I'd say you have yourself a deal, Lord Blackwood.' Jonathan bowed to him.

'Excellent!' The two men shook hands.

Lilah cleared her throat. 'Ahem, are you sure you want to do that? It sounds an awful lot to me and Deborah will benefit from it as well if she marries you.'

Jonathan rounded on her. 'No, she bloody well won't! Every last penny will be used for a stud farm of my own. It will be the best one in England, you'll see. I'm not spending money on fripperies. I daresay Deborah has enough gowns to clothe an army already.'

Lilah and Hamish exchanged an amused glance, but then she grew serious again. 'Please, my lord, won't you tell us your plan?'

'Of course. Here's what we are going to do ...'

Chapter Twelve

When Hamish returned to Deborah at last, he was in a much better mood, but he kept his jubilant thoughts from showing in his expression.

'There you are! What kept you? Is the man dead?' Deborah scowled, then seemed to remember that this wasn't good for her complexion and pushed her fingers across her wrinkled brow in order to smooth it out.

Such compassion, Hamish wanted to say, but instead he replied, 'No, he'll live. It was touch and go though. I've sent for the local surgeon. Should be here shortly. Anyway, Findlay will deal with it now. We have more important matters to discuss.'

'Oh, yes.' Deborah's face lit up and she almost purred when Hamish went up behind her and put his hands on her shoulders, bending down to graze her ear with his lips.

'I've been thinking about what you said, and I do believe you're right. It would be so much easier for me to marry my housekeeper. Then I wouldn't have to pay her and there would be certain other benefits, as you said …' He trailed a finger along her collarbone, making her shiver.

She looked up at him, coquettishly. 'Is that a proposal, my lord? Because if it is, I accept, of course.'

Hamish just smiled, but she didn't notice that he didn't confirm her supposition. 'I do believe this calls for my mother's engagement ring,' he mused, straightening up. 'It's actually a lot more valuable than the one I gave

Deborah, but then she insisted on choosing for herself. Would you mind having my mother's ring, at least for the time being?'

'Oh! Well, it sounds a charming idea. Yes, I think that will do very nicely.'

Good of you. But Hamish didn't say that out loud. He clasped his chin and pretended to think. 'Mother used to keep it in her jewellery box here, so it should still be there. Shall we go and see? Her room has been kept as it was. I didn't have the heart to clear it out, not yet. She only died last year.'

Deborah almost overturned her chair in her haste to stand up. 'Oops!' she giggled happily. 'Yes, do let's. I love a treasure hunt, don't you?'

I'll just bet you do. 'Very exciting. Follow me.'

He led her out of the room and upstairs. His late mother's room was in the keep's only tower, on the second floor, with magnificent views across the loch in almost all directions. He'd been tempted to claim it for himself after her death, as the master bedroom below was much darker.

'Here we are. Now where is that jewellery box?'

Deborah rushed past him, eagerly looking, and almost pounced on a pretty wooden box that sat on his mother's desk. 'Could this be it?' Without asking permission, she opened it, only to stare down at a bundle of letters tied with ribbon.

Hamish had stayed by the door and he smiled at her now. 'Actually, I remember now – the ring is in my safe. And that's where it's staying, *Deborah*.'

He walked out of the room and slammed the door shut, turning the key in the lock.

There was a stunned silence from inside, then a shriek of anger and frustration. 'Lord Blackwood? Hamish? What are you doing? Let me out? You can't ...'

Hamish heard banging on the door and more furious screaming as Deborah realised her ruse had failed. She started shouting, calling him names and swearing vengeance. Hamish shook his head. He wouldn't dignify this with a reply. She deserved none.

'You really think she'll agree?' Lilah was quaking inside, certain that something was going to go wrong with their plan. Hamish's plan.

He shrugged. 'Probably not, but it's up to her, the offer will be there. At the very least we can undo the damage she's already done.'

They had all travelled to Gretna Green in Hamish's carriage, with Deborah alternately ranting at them and sulking. It had been a very uncomfortable journey and they'd been glad to reach the inn, where Jonathan was currently in charge of making sure Deborah stayed in the private parlour they'd bespoken.

Hamish had asked Lilah to go for a walk with him to get some air before they set off for the smithy to hopefully put matters right.

'Morwell has promised to make sure your sister doesn't escape,' he told her once they were outside the inn. 'We can have a short break from her nonsense. Come.'

He held out his arm for her to take now and she placed her fingers on it carefully. She found it difficult to be so close to him, touching him even through the material of his coat sleeve. She was extremely aware of him – the way he smiled, how handsome he was, the lovely scent of his shaving soap – it made her tingle all over as if there was some sort of lightning current between them. It was silly, she knew it, but couldn't seem to stop her body from reacting to him in this way. Lilah turned her head away as she felt her cheeks turn warm.

They walked a little way along a country lane until they were out of sight of any buildings. Hamish stopped and turned to her, removing her fingers from his arm and taking hold of both her hands instead. 'Delilah, I need to speak to you about something.'

'Wh-what?' She was wearing gloves, but still felt the warmth of his hands on hers.

'I've decided I don't want you to be my housekeeper any more.'

Lilah took a deep breath to steady herself as she almost reeled physically from this blow. It did feel as though someone had punched her, hard, in the stomach and she had trouble making her lungs function. 'But I thought I'd managed things very well,' she protested. 'Are you not satisfied with the way I've run the house? Should I have made the servants work harder?'

'No, no, you've done very well. I can't fault your housekeeping skills as such.'

'What then? Is it the others? Have they complained because I'm too young? I honestly don't see that it should make a difference as long as I'm capable of—'

'Delilah.' He put one finger across her lips to stop her in mid-sentence and the slight contact stunned her into silence. 'You've done nothing wrong. The fact is, it's me. I simply can't have such a beautiful young lady around the place, tempting me to … well, tempting me. Do you see?'

Lilah swallowed down a sob which wanted to escape and nodded. 'Yes.'

What was she to do now? Perhaps he could at least give her a good reference. She opened her mouth to ask, but he forestalled her.

'Forgive me, I'm not telling you the whole truth. What I'm trying to lead up to is that I don't want you as my housekeeper, but I would like you in another role.'

Lilah gasped. *No!* She didn't want to be anyone's mistress. That was what she'd been trying to avoid, surely he knew that? She'd rather work much harder, in any menial capacity. She shook her head.

Hamish smiled. 'Hear me out, please. Delilah, beautiful, amazing Delilah, would you do me the honour of becoming my wife?'

Lilah felt as if all the air whooshed out of her and she almost crumpled – with relief, surprise, astonishment. 'Wife? You want to marry me? Your housekeeper?'

He put his hand on her cheek and stroked the soft skin with his thumb. 'You're a lady, Delilah, no matter what. And yes, I would very much like to marry you, if you think you could bear it?'

'I … of course. I mean, I would like nothing better, but, why? I would have thought you'd had more than enough of my family by now.'

His hand stayed where it was and she wanted to lean into it, surrender herself to him on any terms, but she also wanted to know why he was proposing now. Did he feel sorry for her, after what Deborah had tried to do?

Hamish smiled. 'The rest of them can go hang, as far as I'm concerned, but you have definitely grown on me. For you, I have nothing but the utmost respect, the deepest love. That's the truth – I love you, Lilah, and I can't imagine my life without you now.' A small frown appeared between his eyebrows. 'If you don't feel the same way though, I'd never force you. I know you said you weren't looking for marriage.'

'That wasn't quite true.' Lilah looked up at him and dared to smile back as his words allayed her fears. 'I just didn't want to marry anyone other than you, and I thought the chances of that were very slim.'

'I did offer.'

'Only because you thought I was blackmailing you. I didn't want you on those terms.' Lilah didn't add that it had taken all her willpower to refuse, but she'd known he would never love her if she forced him, the way Deborah had done.

'That's why I love you – unlike your sister, you have principles.' Hamish's smile widened. 'So what do you say, shall we marry today, at the smithy? I, for one, don't want to wait another second.'

Lilah laughed. 'Yes, please, if you're sure?'

'I've never been more sure of anything in my life.'

Her happiness dimmed slightly. 'We might have trouble persuading the smith to marry me to someone again though, since he thinks he's already done it once.'

'Don't worry, I'm sure we can make him see sense. Let's go and put the first part of our plan into action, then we'll see.' He put his arms around her. 'But before we go, there's something I've been wanting to do again for a very long time.'

Lilah didn't have a chance to protest as he bent to kiss her, softly, gently, thoroughly. But then she didn't want to because it was what she'd dreamed of every night since the first time he'd done it and she couldn't believe it was actually happening at last.

She was the luckiest woman on earth.

Delilah took a deep breath and walked into the smithy at Gretna Green. Jonathan was already there, holding onto a furious-looking Deborah whom he'd more or less dragged in there a few moments earlier.

'I say, what's this then? Didn't want to let yer sister be the only one married, eh?' the smith said when he caught sight of them, grinning at his own joke, although he was looking from one girl to the other as though he wasn't quite sure which one of them to address.

'Just so.' Hamish nodded. 'Only, there's been a slight mistake and we've come to rectify it. I do hope you can help us?'

'I don't see why not. What can I do for ye?'

'The fact of the matter is that this lady,' Hamish indicated Deborah, 'pretended to be her sister when she married Mr Morwell the other day. Would you say the marriage is valid under such circumstances?'

The smith frowned. 'Er, no, I don't suppose so. I mean, there must be people givin' a false name on occasion, for nefarious purposes like, but I've never heard of anyone marryin' instead of their sister.'

'Good. Then perhaps you'd be so kind as to cross out that entry from your records and write "marriage null and void" or some such thing next to it?'

'He's lying.' Deborah raised her voice. 'It's just that

my stupid twin has changed her mind and decided she doesn't want to be married to Mr Morwell any longer.'

'Eh? But ...' The smith, who'd been in the process of opening his ledger, looked confused. 'Can ye prove it?'

'Don't listen to her,' Jonathan put in. 'She's the one who is lying. I was aware of her true identity at the time of the marriage and I'm ashamed to say I aided and abetted her in this deceit. Her name is not Delilah, as she claimed, it's Deborah – I've known these ladies since childhood and I assure you I can tell them apart so I was fully aware which one of them stood beside me that day.'

'There are three of us against one,' Hamish put in, his voice quietly authoritative. We'd all be prepared to sign an affidavit to that effect if you like? Or swear on the Bible, whichever you prefer.'

The smith glared at Deborah, whose face was twisted into an ugly expression, and shook his head. 'No, I don't believe that will be necessary. I can see she's a hellcat.'

'Why you ...!' Deborah tried to lunge for the man but was held back by Jonathan's strong grip on her arm.

'What of the marriage lines I gave ye?' the smith asked Jonathan.

'I burned that document,' Lilah told him.

'Yes, she did,' Jonathan confirmed.

'Excellent.' The smith found the entry in his ledger and crossed it out with a thick line of black ink, making a note in the margin. 'That's that then.'

Hamish pulled a fat purse out of his pocket but the smith waved it away, obviously an honest man.

'No need for that. I'm happy to have cleared up the mistake.'

'Thank you.' Hamish bowed, then turned to Jonathan. 'You had a proposition, I believe?'

Jonathan nodded, looking more determined than Lilah had ever seen him. He took Deborah's hand and held onto it, even though she tried to pull away from him. 'Deborah, we have always been friends, despite everything, and I would be happy to marry you, here and now, in order to save *your* reputation. What you did, or tried to do, to Lilah was despicable and I'm sure you won't want it to become known. But I'm prepared to overlook it as I'm sure you had your reasons. People will wonder where you've been and there may be someone who saw us leave together. I'm offering you the protection of my name if you'll have me. That way we can say we were eloping to Gretna and everyone will stop talking about you and Blackwood eventually.'

Deborah's eyes widened. 'Marry you? Over my dead body. I can do so much better than that, just you wait and see.'

Jonathan flinched and his mouth tightened, but he didn't react to the insult in any other way. 'Well, think it over for a few moments. I believe you're wrong and the offer is there.'

Deborah turned her back on him, crossing her arms over her chest. 'Just leave me alone, you traitor. If it wasn't for your cowardice, Lilah would still legally be your wife now.'

'Doing the right thing does not equate with being a coward, but fine, have it your way,' Jonathan said.

'Then if you wouldn't mind, sir, could you marry us instead?' Hamish said to the smith, taking Lilah's hand to pull her forward. 'I do believe this lady is willing, at least.'

She felt her cheeks turn rosy, but smiled up at him. 'Definitely.'

Lilah heard her sister's gasp and a strangled expletive, but didn't look that way. She didn't want Deborah's sour expression to ruin this most perfect moment.

'I refuse to be a witness to this,' Deborah hissed.

'I'll fetch my apprentice then,' the smith said. 'We do need two witnesses after all. I'm assumin' the gentleman won't mind?' He looked at Jonathan, who nodded.

'I'd be happy to oblige.'

After the brief ceremony, the smith held out the ledger to Lilah. 'Here ye go, then, if ye wouldnae mind signin' – again as it were.' The man smiled. 'I do hope we have the right lady this time 'cos I'm not changin' it further.'

Lilah wrote her name. 'No, I promise you I am definitely Delilah. Thank you.'

They repaired back to the nearby inn and entered their private parlour. Hamish turned to Deborah. 'Are you sure you don't want to take Mr Morwell up on his offer before we leave? I sincerely doubt you'll receive a better one any time soon.'

Deborah replied with something very rude, which Lilah thought she must have overheard the stable boys saying.

Hamish shook his head. 'Language! Whoever he may be, your future husband will need to teach you some manners.'

'I very much doubt that's possible,' Jonathan muttered.

'Can I have a word with you in private, please?' Hamish said to him. 'Let's go outside for a moment.'

The two men left the room and Lilah stayed behind to make sure Deborah didn't go anywhere. She didn't think her sister could get up to any more mischief now, but she wasn't taking any chances.

'I suppose you're going to gloat now,' Deborah sneered. 'But I'll get you back for this so don't count your chickens just yet.'

Lilah didn't reply. What was there to say after all? Her sister would never change.

Chapter Thirteen

'Deborah! Delilah? And ... Lord Blackwood? What is the meaning of this? I hadn't thought to see you back here, sir. Young Morwell?'

Lord and Lady Risden had been in the drawing room, in the middle of an argument if the sounds coming through the door were anything to go by. Both looked astonished to see their daughters arriving back together, and with two men in tow.

'Lilah, where on earth have you been?' Lady Risden stood up and fixed them all with a glare. She looked as though she'd been crying, her eyes red-rimmed as she clutched a handkerchief. 'I've been worried sick about you. And as for you, Deborah, how could you go off like that, with just your maid for company? Honestly, have you both run mad?'

'I can explain, Lady Risden,' Hamish cut in, not wanting any histrionics. He'd had quite enough of those from Deborah during the journey. 'Delilah has been under my protection—'

'I say, really, my lord!' Lord Risden cut in, his face turning quite puce with indignation. 'That's no way to treat my—'

Hamish held up a hand to stop him saying anything further. 'As my wife. Delilah is Lady Blackwood now so there is no impropriety, I assure you.'

'There was though ...' Deborah muttered, but when Hamish threw her a cold glare she closed her mouth.

'Delilah is? Well, I never!' Lady Risden smiled, obviously delighted at the news that one of her girls had managed to snare the earl at last. But then her smile faded. 'What about Deborah then? I thought she said she was going to …'

'Mama!' Deborah hissed. 'Not now.'

'Oh.'

Hamish continued as if he hadn't been interrupted. 'Deborah is not married, my lady, but as she and Mr Morwell travelled in the company of Dawson, her maid, there is no cause for scandal there either.' He glanced at Jonathan. 'I believe she had intended for Delilah to marry Mr Morwell, but since Lilah was already spoken for … When they found out, he did offer to marry Deborah instead but she's refused him so that's that.'

Lord Risden frowned. 'That's all a mite confusing, Blackwood, if you don't mind me saying so. Why would Deborah go haring off to … where have you been, exactly?'

'Gretna Green,' Hamish supplied.

'I told you in the note I left you,' Deborah added, but her father wasn't listening.

'Right, to Gretna, with a young man she wanted her sister to marry? Doesn't make sense to me.'

'I was trying to be helpful, Papa. By getting Jonathan to marry Lilah, I was saving her from being ostracised.'

'Fustian!' Lilah, Hamish and Jonathan exclaimed at the same time.

Lord Risden's scowl grew as he regarded the four of them. 'I think I see more clearly now.' He fixed Deborah with a stern gaze. 'You've been up to your tricks again, haven't you, my girl?

'No, Papa.' Deborah stepped forward and went over to her father, winding her arms around one of his. 'I'm very sorry I went on my little journey without asking permission, but I did take Dawson with me as my chaperone, as Lord Blackwood said. And you know I needed Lilah to come back and tell everyone she was mistaken. I explained it all in my note.'

'Well, I couldn't make head nor tail of it, I have to admit,' Lord Risden said. 'And are you sure Lilah was mistaken? You never gave Lord Blackwood laudanum?'

'Perhaps just a very tiny amount, Papa, but he was going to offer for me in any case so I was just making sure that—'

'I was not!' Hamish interjected. 'Beg your pardon, sir, but nothing on earth would have induced me to marry your daughter if I hadn't been forced into it. I wasn't in the market for a wife at all at the time.'

Lord Risden stared down at his daughter. 'So you admit to putting laudanum in his lordship's drink?'

'Yes, a little, as I said, but it was a mere trifle.'

Her father shook his head. 'No, Deborah. It was the straw that broke the camel's back.'

'What do you mean?'

'For years I have put up with your machinations, your tantrums, your manipulation, but no more. You went too far when you compromised a peer of the realm, an earl no less, and forced him to the altar. I'm sorry, but I admire Delilah for telling the world the truth and standing up for what was right, even though it has caused our family a great deal of scandal. But no more.'

'Papa! Lilah was just jealous. She was in love with Lord Blackwood, don't you see? So much so that she lied and said he'd seduced her. In fact, she's always been jealous of me, you know she has.'

'Be that as it may – and if you knew her to be in love with his lordship, that makes your behaviour even worse, by the way – she acted honourably, if somewhat unwisely, and for that I commend her. As for you, Deborah, you have made your own bed and now you must lie in it, as young Morwell's wife.'

'What? No! I—'

He cut her off. 'It seems to me you'd better accept young Jonathan's suit after all. A quiet country wedding sounds just the thing to stop all the tongues wagging. No offence, young man,' he said to Jonathan, 'but you weren't quite the catch I'd had in mind for my girls. Still, I know your father well and perhaps we can come to some agreement so that he gives you some of the land that abuts my property.'

'Hold on a moment. You can't be serious, Papa! I don't want to marry Jon and it's not necessary. It'll all blow over in no time, you'll see.'

To Hamish's relief Lord Risden stood firm. 'No, enough is enough. There will be no more London seasons for you in any case, so you may as well marry now or else remain on the shelf. Young Morwell will be a good husband, I'm sure, and you'd better be a good wife to him or I'll make sure you live in penury for the rest of your life. Do I make myself clear?'

Hamish almost laughed out loud. The expression on Deborah's face was one of horror and utter disbelief. He doubted anyone had spoken to her thus in her entire life, apart from himself. True to form, his new sister-in-law tried to cajole her way out of her predicament with tears next, but that had no effect either. Lord Risden cut her short.

'For heaven's sake, girl, go to your room if you're going to make all that noise. The rest of us don't want to hear it. And don't come out until you're ready to act like a proper lady and accompany Jonathan home to tell his parents the good news. I might even go with you myself. Then we can go and have a word with the vicar.'

Deborah shrieked with frustration, but eventually fled the room and silence reigned.

'Are you sure you can handle her?' Lord Risden finally said to Jonathan. 'She is a bit of a handful.'

'Oh, don't worry, sir, I've known her since we were knee-high to a grasshopper. She'll come round. In the meantime, I've plenty to do with my horses.'

Lord Risden clapped him on the back. 'Good man. We'll see about setting you up with some better facilities, eh?'

'Er, thank you, my lord, that would be marvellous!'

'Let's discuss it after dinner. But now, I believe you would all like to freshen up, no? I'll ring for the Jackson. No doubt he'll have organised rooms for you by now. Splendid fellow. You'll stay the night, won't you, Jonathan?'

Lilah had never been so glad to escape to her room as she was now, but at the same time she felt nervous because she was to share it with her new husband. They hadn't slept together during the journey because she'd had to share a room with Deborah and her maid.

'We don't want her setting off on her own and causing any more mayhem,' Hamish had told her, and added in a whisper, 'And it's probably for the best anyway as I don't want our first night together to be spoiled in any way.'

But now the time had come. Would Hamish regret having married her? She knew she was naive when it came to men and didn't have the first idea how to please him.

'Lilah, what's the matter? You're not sorry you married me, are you?' Hamish had come up behind her as she stood by the window staring out into the darkness, her arms wrapped around herself.

'No, of course not, but … I was wondering if you regretted it? I … what if you don't like me once we've … you know.'

Hamish turned her around, gently. 'Lilah, look at me, please.' She did and was amazed to find his eyes shining as he smiled. 'I will never regret it, ever, I promise you. And tonight I will show you that there is nothing whatsoever for you to worry about. I can guarantee I won't be disappointed and I hope you won't be either. There's just one thing – you haven't actually told me you love me. Was I wrong in thinking that?'

'No, oh no. I do love you, with all my heart. I have done from the first time I saw you, I think, and it must have been very obvious since Deborah found out so easily. I just couldn't believe it would ever be reciprocated. Can't believe it now.'

'Lilah, my love, don't ever doubt it. I must have been blind not to have noticed you, but now I have and there's no one else who could ever take your place. I love you, my beautiful wife, more than I can say. Let me show you instead, tonight and always. Deborah can never come between us again, I swear.'

Lilah was happy to let him prove it to her for the rest of her life.

Epilogue

Hamish stood in front of the altar of the small country church once more, but this time he didn't feel trapped and had no wish whatsoever to run away. He put his hand over that of his lovely wife's, which was resting in the crook of his arm, and gave it a reassuring squeeze.

They'd decided they may as well have their marriage blessed by the church at the same time as Deborah and Jonathan became man and wife. Their Gretna marriage was legal and binding, since they'd both consented to it and had taken their vows in front of witnesses, but Hamish had felt the need to do things properly, for Lilah's sake and to show the world that this time he hadn't been coerced.

He smiled down at her and bent to brush her cheek with his lips. She smiled back, happiness and love for him shining out of those amazing silver-coloured eyes. He couldn't believe he could be this lucky.

'There are hardly any flowers. I asked for lots! I can't believe Papa is being so stingy. And why can't we have more guests? It's downright miserly, I tell you ...'

Deborah and Jonathan stood beside Hamish and Delilah, and Deborah had been muttering complaints ever since they'd left the Risden's manor house. Her dress was apparently 'paltry', her bouquet too small and not scented enough, her bonnet should have had more trimmings and her shoes pinched. The list was endless, but no one had paid her any attention and when the vicar cleared his throat, her litany finally dwindled and came to a halt. Perhaps she realised, at last, that her fate was sealed and there was absolutely nothing she could do about it.

Hamish and Lilah shared a look of amusement and both glanced at Jonathan, who seemed calm and unfazed. 'He's probably thinking about that new stallion he bought yesterday, it fits perfectly in the stables of his new estate,' Hamish whispered, and saw Lilah struggle to keep from giggling out loud.

'Shhh,' she whispered back. 'Behave yourself!' But her eyes were dancing and Hamish knew she'd been thinking the same thing.

Jonathan had proved extremely single-minded, and once it became clear he would have the stud farm and breeding stock he'd always dreamed of, none of Deborah's tantrums or complaints appeared to have any effect on him. It was as though he was living in a bubble of happiness and contentment that nothing could pierce. Well, good for him, Hamish thought.

'Ahem, we are gathered here today …' the vicar began, then hesitated and threw a wary glance in Hamish's direction as if he wondered what would go wrong this time.

But Hamish was determined that nothing would mar this occasion and he had no intention of leaving until his and Lilah's marriage was blessed. He gave the vicar a blinding smile and nodded at him to proceed.

This time, he was exactly where he wanted to be.

About the Author

Christina lives near Hereford and is married with two children. Although born in England she has a Swedish mother and was brought up in Sweden. In her teens, the family moved to Japan where she had the opportunity to travel extensively in the Far East.

Christina's debut *Trade Winds* was short listed for the 2011 Romantic Novelists' Association's Pure Passion Award for Best Historical Fiction. *The Scarlet Kimono* won the 2011 Big Red Reads Best Historical Fiction Award. *Highland Storms* (in 2012) and *The Gilded Fan* (in 2014) won the Best Historical Romantic Novel of the year award and *The Silent Touch of Shadows* won the 2012 Best Historical Read Award from the Festival of Romance.

For more information on Christina:
www.twitter.com/PiaCCourtenay
www.christinacourtenay.com
www.facebook.com/christinacourtenayauthor

More Choc Lit

From Christina Courtenay

The Silent Touch of Shadows

Book 1 in the Shadows from the Past series

Winner of the 2012 Best Historical Read from the Festival of Romance

What will it take to put the past to rest? Professional genealogist Melissa Grantham receives an invitation to visit her family's ancestral home, Ashleigh Manor. From the moment she arrives, life-like dreams and visions haunt her. The spiritual connection to a medieval young woman and her forbidden lover have her questioning her sanity, but Melissa is determined to solve the mystery.

A haunting love story set partly in the present and partly in fifteenth century Kent.

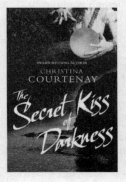

The Secret Kiss of Darkness

Book 2 in the Shadows from the Past series

Must forbidden love end in heartbreak? Kayla Sinclair knows she's in big trouble when she almost bankrupts herself to buy a life-size portrait of a mysterious eighteenth century man at an auction. Jago Kerswell, inn-keeper and smuggler, knows there is danger in those stolen moments with Lady Eliza Marcombe, but he'll take any risk to be with her.

Forbidden love, smugglers and romance!

The Soft Whisper of Dreams

Book 3 in the Shadows from the Past series

Some dreams shouldn't come true …
Maddie Browne thought she'd grown out
of the recurring nightmare that plagued
her as a child, but after a shocking
family secret is revealed, it comes back to
haunt her – the same swing in the same
garden, the kind red-haired giant and
the swarthy arms which grab her from
behind and try to take her away …

In an attempt to forget her troubles,
Maddie travels to Devon to spend
time with her friends, Kayla and
Wes. However, it becomes clear that
relaxation will not be on the agenda
after a disturbing encounter with a
gypsy fortune teller. Not to mention the
presence of Wes's dangerously handsome
brother, Alex.

The Velvet Cloak of Moonlight

Book 4 in the Shadows from the Past Series

**"As the velvet cloak of moonlight settled
over the ruined towers of Raglan Castle,
the shadows beneath them stirred …"**
When newly widowed Tess visits Raglan
Castle, she experiences an extraordinary
vision that transports her to a
seventeenth-century Wales and a castle
on the brink of a siege.

Even when Tess leaves Raglan to
return to Merrick Court, her late
husband's home, the strange dreams
continue as her life becomes increasingly
intertwined with the past. And when the
new owner of the estate arrives – New
Zealander Josh Owens – the parallels
become even more obvious.

But perhaps the visions aren't just
trying to tell their own story, maybe
they're also giving a warning …

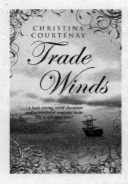

Trade Winds

Book 1 in the Kinross series

Shortlisted for the 2011 Pure Passion Award for Best Romantic Historical Fiction

Marriage of convenience or a love for life?
It's 1732 in Gothenburg, Sweden, and strong-willed Jess van Sandt knows only too well that it's a man's world. She believes she's being swindled out of her inheritance by her stepfather – and she's determined to stop it.

When help appears in the unlikely form of handsome Scotsman Killian Kinross, Jess finds herself both intrigued and infuriated by him. In an attempt to recover her fortune, she proposes a marriage of convenience. Then Killian is offered the chance of a lifetime with the Swedish East India Company's Expedition and he's determined that nothing will stand in his way, not even his new bride.

Highland Storms

Book 2 in the Kinross series

Winner of the 2012 Best Historical Romantic Novel of the year

Who can you trust?
Betrayed by his brother and his childhood love, Brice Kinross needs a fresh start. So he welcomes the opportunity to leave Sweden for the Scottish Highlands to take over the family estate.

But there's trouble afoot at Rosyth in 1754. The estate's in ruin and money is disappearing. He discovers an ally in Marsaili Buchanan, the beautiful red-headed housekeeper, but can he trust her?

Marsaili works hard at being a housekeeper and harder still at avoiding men who want to take advantage of her. But she's irresistibly drawn to the new clan chief, even though he's made it plain he doesn't want to be shackled to anyone.

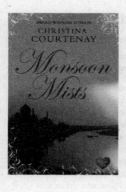

Monsoon Mists

Book 3 in the Kinross series

Sometimes the most precious things cannot be bought ...
It's 1759 and Jamie Kinross has travelled far to escape his troubled past – from the pine forests of Sweden to the bustling streets of India.

In India he starts a new life as a gem trader, but when his mentor's family are kidnapped as part of a criminal plot, he vows to save them and embarks on a dangerous mission to the city of Surat, carrying the stolen talisman of an Indian Rajah.

There he encounters Zarmina Miller. She is rich and beautiful, but her infamous haughtiness has earned her a nickname: The Ice Widow. Jamie is instantly tempted by the challenge she presents.

The Scarlet Kimono

Book 1 in the Kumashiro Series

Winner of the 2011 Big Red Read's Best Historical Fiction Award

Abducted by a Samurai warlord in 17th-century Japan – what happens when fear turns to love?
England, 1611, and young Hannah Marston envies her brother's adventurous life. But when she stows away on his merchant ship, her powers of endurance are stretched to their limit. Then they reach Japan and all her suffering seems worthwhile – until she is abducted by Taro Kumashiro's warriors.

In the far north of the country, warlord Kumashiro is waiting to see the girl who he has been warned about by a seer. When at last they meet, it's a clash of cultures and wills, but they're also fighting an instant attraction to each other.

The Gilded Fan

Book 2 in the Kumashiro Series

Winner of the 2014 Romantic Historical Novel Award

How do you start a new life, leaving behind all you love?

It's 1641, and when Midori Kumashiro, the orphaned daughter of a warlord, is told she has to leave Japan or die, she has no choice but to flee to England. Midori is trained in the arts of war, but is that enough to help her survive a journey, with a lecherous crew and an attractive captain she doesn't trust?

Having come to Nagasaki to trade, the last thing Captain Nico Noordholt wants is a female passenger, especially a beautiful one. How can he protect her from his crew when he can't keep his own eyes off her?

The Jade Lioness

Book 3 in the Kumashiro Series

Can an impossible love become possible?

Nagasaki, 1648

Temperance Marston longs to escape war-torn England and explore the exotic empire of Japan. When offered the chance to accompany her cousin and Captain Noordholt on a trading expedition to Nagasaki, she jumps at the opportunity. However, she soon finds the country's strict laws for foreigners curtail her freedom.

On a dangerous and foolhardy venture she meets Kazuo, a ronin. Long ago, his father was accused of a crime he didn't commit – stealing a valuable jade lioness ornament from the Shogun – and Kazuo must restore his family's honour. But when Temperance is kidnapped and sold as a concubine, he has to make a decision – can he save her and keep the promise he made to his father?

Marry in Haste

Book 1 in the Regency Romance Collection

'I need to marry, and I need to marry at once'

When James, Viscount Demarr confides in an acquaintance at a ball one evening, he has no idea that the potential solution to his problems stands so close at hand ...

Amelia Ravenscroft is the granddaughter of a earl and is desperate to escape her aunt's home where she has endured a life of drudgery, whilst fighting off the increasingly bold advances of her lecherous cousin. She boldly proposes a marriage of convenience.

And Amelia soon proves herself a perfect fit for the role of Lady Demarr. But James has doubts and his blossoming feelings are blighted by suspicions regarding Amelia's past.

Will they find, all too painfully, that if you marry in haste you repent at leisure?

Once Bitten, Twice Shy

Book 2 in the Regency Romance Collection

'Once was more than enough!'

Jason Warwycke, Marquess of Wyckeham, has vowed never to wed again after his disastrous first marriage, which left him with nothing but a tarnished reputation and a rather unfortunate nickname – 'Lord Wicked'.

That is, until he sets eyes on Ianthe Templeton ...

But can Wyckeham and Ianthe overcome the malicious schemes of spiteful siblings and evil stepmothers to find wedded bliss? Or will Wyckeham discover, all too painfully, that the past has come back to bite him for a second time?

Desperate Remedies

Book 3 in the Regency Romance Collection

'She would never forget the day her heart broke ...'

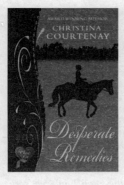

Lexie Holloway falls desperately in love with the devastatingly handsome Earl of Synley after a brief encounter at a ball. But Synley is already engaged to be married and scandal surrounds his unlikely match with the ageing, but incredibly wealthy, Lady Catherine Downes. Heartbroken, Lexie resolves to remain a spinster and allows circumstance to carry her far away from England to a new life in Italy. However, the dashing Earl is never far from her thoughts.

Can Lexie help Synley outwit those who wish to harm him and rekindle the flame ignited all those years ago, or will her associations with the Earl bring her nothing but trouble?

Never Too Late

Book 4 in the Regency Romance Collection

Can true love be rekindled?

Maude is devastated when the interference of her strict father prevents her from eloping with Luke Hexham. It is not long before she is married off to Edward, Luke's cousin – a good match in her father's eyes but an abhorrent one to his daughter.

Eight years later, Edward is dead. Maude, now Lady Hexham, is appalled to find his entire estate is to go to Luke – the man she still loves – with no provision for either herself or her young daughter. Luke has never forgotten Maude's apparent betrayal, but he has the means to help her.

Soon Maude and Luke realise that perhaps it is never too late for true love.

New England Rocks

Book 1 in the Northbrooke High series

First impressions, how wrong can you get?
When Rain Mackenzie is expelled from
her British boarding school, she can't
believe her bad luck. Not only is she
forced to move to New England, USA,
she's also sent to the local high school, as
a punishment.

Rain makes it her mission to dislike
everything about Northbrooke High,
but what she doesn't bank on is meeting
Jesse Devlin …

Jesse is the hottest guy Rain's ever seen
and he plays guitar in an awesome rock
band!

There's just one small problem … Jesse
already has a girlfriend, little miss perfect
Amber Lawrence, who looks set to cause
trouble as Rain and Jesse grow closer.

But, what does it matter? New
England sucks anyway, and Rain doesn't
plan on sticking around …

Does she?

A young adult novel

Introducing Choc Lit

We're an independent publisher creating
a delicious selection of fiction.
Where heroes are like chocolate – irresistible!
Quality stories with a romance at the heart.

See our selection here:
www.choc-lit.com

We'd love to hear how you enjoyed *Marry for Love*
from our Choc Lit Taster range. Please leave a
review where you purchased the novel or visit:
www.choc-lit.com and give your feedback.

Choc Lit novels are selected by genuine readers like yourself.
We only publish stories our Choc Lit Tasting Panel want to see
in print. Our reviews and awards speak for themselves.

Could you be a Star Selector and join our Tasting Panel?
Would you like to play a role in choosing which novels we
decide to publish? Do you enjoy reading romance novels?
Then you could be perfect for our Choc Lit Tasting Panel.

Visit here for more details…
www.choc-lit.com/join-the-choc-lit-tasting-panel

Keep in touch:
Sign up for our monthly newsletter Choc Lit Spread for all
the latest news and offers: www.spread.choc-lit.com.
Follow us on Twitter: @ChocLituk and Facebook: Choc Lit.

Where heroes are like chocolate – irresistible!